ANGEL OF RECKONING

RECLAIMING HONOR BOOK 04

JUSTIN SLOAN
MICHAEL ANDERLE

COPYRIGHT

LMBPN Publishing
PMB 196, 2540 South Maryland Pkwy
Las Vegas, NV 89109

First US edition, 2017
Version 1.01 Edition April 2017

DEDICATION

From Justin
To Ugulay, Verona and Brendan Sloan
From Michael
To Family, Friends and
Those Who Love
To Read.
May We All Enjoy Grace
To Live The Life We Are
Called.

Angel of Reckoning
Reclaiming Honor Team

Beta Editor / Readers
Robin Heath
Beck Young
Erin McNutty
Lori Owens
Lee Balta
Trista Collins
Nipa Jhaveri
JIT Beta Readers
Alex Wilson
Kimberly Boyer
Brent Bakken
Micky Cocker
Ginger Sparkman
Bruce Loving
John Raisor

If I missed anyone, please let me know!

Editors
Stephen Russell
Thank you to the following Special Consultants
Jeff Morris - US Army - Asst Professor Cyber-Warfare, Nuclear Munitions (Active)
W.W.D.E

CHAPTER ONE

Old Manhattan, Sandra's Café

"I must die," Valerie said.

Neither Sandra nor Jackson seemed to hear her. Sandra was too busy arranging a cheese and wine sampler that some of her customers had ordered, while Jackson stood at the entryway to the backroom where they were all huddled. He kept pulling the curtain aside and nervously glancing out.

Valerie looked over her shoulder at Diego, going through one of the crates of supplies that had recently been delivered via blimp from Europe.

"Thank God this shipment made it through," he said, closing the lid and turning to them with a smile. "All accounted for."

"Good." Sandra sliced chunks of cheese from a block, but this last one she held as if she was going to take a bite. But right when it was close to her mouth she pulled it back to say, "One more damn shipment intercepted by those pirates, and

I swear to god I'll figure out how to become a vampire and go after them myself."

Valerie just shook her head, flabbergasted.

"What?" Sandra asked. She looked at the others, who looked equally confused. "Did we miss something?"

"Only my death." Valerie rolled her eyes. "But no one cares about that, apparently."

"As far as I'm concerned, you're invincible," Diego said.

Jackson let the curtain fall and looked back at her. "Dear, the people of this city, those that know anything about you anyway, love you. They'd follow you to the ends of the earth."

"And yet, none of that changes the fact that I *have* to die," Valerie said. She stood now, brushing out her purple coat over the tight leather outfit she had become accustomed to wearing. She mostly moved in the shadows and stayed out of sight anyway.

So why not wear what made her feel sexy and badass?

This got their attention, and Sandra took a swig of a nearby glass of wine, but then realized she wasn't supposed to. She shrugged and drank the rest from the glass.

They were all looking at Valerie, waiting.

"It's like this," she said, "the three amigos will keep sending assassins after me, and—"

"Wait, three amigos?" Jackson turned from his post to look at her. "You're bringing that back?"

"Back?" Diego asked.

Valerie leaned against the counter, knowingly. "It was what a lot of the Enforcers and others called them before we ousted Strake. Referring to the CEOs, of course. The point is, we've taken out at least ten of their assassins since that night at the Bazaar, right? And who knows how many others they have in reserve, or what sort of sick game they want to play next. For all I know, they'll come after you three."

"Which is why you aren't seen with us," Sandra said.

"I wish it were so simple." Valerie stood and walked over to Jackson, waving. She pulled back the curtain slightly. "See that man in the corner, the one who keeps glancing out of the window. Yeah, one of them. A vampire, so I'm willing to bet Forsaken, and likely one of these new assassins, just waiting for me to come walking by."

She let the curtain drop and turned to the group. "So you see, I have to die. Well, fake die, anyway, so that they think I'm dead."

"Won't that be dangerous for the city, though?" Jackson asked. "I mean, if they think you're out of the picture, what's to stop them from just coming back here with their army and moving in?"

"Honestly, I think we did a number on their army," she replied. "And this city has Cammie, Royland, you Jackson, and the police force. The city is in damn-good hands. And then there's the fact that, if they think I'm dead, they'll be extra surprised when I show up on their doorsteps to bring them justice."

"You want to go after them?" Jackson was staring at her now with wide, uncertain eyes.

"It's the only way to truly end this."

She turned then and walked out the back, taking the secret route. She sensed their confused emotions as she walked away. It swept over her like a cold tingling, and then she was in the alley and it was gone.

Glancing at the nearby streets to ensure no one else was watching her, she then walked over to stop at the corner, just within sight of the people from inside, glanced around, and waited. It was dark out, so she wanted to be sure the assassin saw her, and then she walked back into the alley.

A moment later, she heard the door close and shoes scuff on concrete, but when the Forsaken she had smelled entered the alley, his expression darkened at the fact that he was, seemingly, alone.

Then the fear hit him, but only slightly, as Valerie couldn't control its direction and didn't want to scare off the customers within Sandra's café.

The Forsaken took a step back, eyes wide and darting back and forth across the alley, but before he could take another step back, she was on him, swooping down from behind with a strike so hard he went flying into the brick wall on the other side.

But this one was better than the last the CEOs had sent after her, and a split-second after impact he had rolled aside, pulled out two silver-plated blades, and slashed, knowing she would have come in for the attack.

The son of a bitch was right, and dammit the tiny cut on the tip of her knuckle hurt. While she had gotten more used to pain with all of it that she had to deal with over the past couple of months in Old Manhattan, she still hated it just as much. She just had a higher threshold for it than most.

So when she blocked the next strike and kicked out his knee, she kicked it with such ferocity that not only did she bust the kneecap, but she sent her foot straight through it.

It was disgusting.

The Forsaken stared at her for a second, then lunged as she tried to step back… but he collapsed right onto his face.

"They need to train you bastards for years before sending you out here like this," Valerie said as she knelt next to him, ignoring his groans and his writhing of pain. She took one of the blades, which he had dropped in his fall, and put it to his throat. “I wish I could tell you to run off, to warn your masters that their days are numbered, but…” She glanced over at the severed leg and cringed. “That really is disgusting. You should see someone about that.” And then she put an end to him. She tossed the body into an old dumpster that smelled like rotten diapers left out for years, and went back into the café.

She immediately went to the service sink and washed her hands, annoyed that they had a red stain that was harder to get off than she had hoped. Before the others had a chance to ask her what that was all about, a quick knock came from the wall next to the curtain.

“Yes?” Sandra asked.

“The guy who ordered the crème brûlée is gone,” the waitress Sandra had hired said, sticking her head in the back. “Anyone want it?”

Valerie raised an eyebrow and said, “Over here.” She smiled as the waitress handed it over, and then broke the hard top with her spoon, already loving the sweet scent of cream and vanilla. When she noticed Sandra staring at her, she said, “What? It’s not like it goes to my hips or anything.” She took a bite and moaned. “Oh God, this is definitely one of the best perks of being a vampire. No need to stress over what I’m eating.”

“You’re telling me you could eat straight sugar for a week and not have any concerns?”

She thought about it. “I imagine I still need nutrients, but the negatives? Yeah, I’m pretty sure my body would fight it off.” After another bite, she said, “Oh, yeah, we’re going to need some people to clean up the alley. A bit of a mess.”

“Please try to keep it away from the café,” Sandra said, exasperated.

"Hey, tell the idiots to attack me somewhere else and..." A thought hit her, and she frowned. "Shit, they're coming here, looking for me. Sandra, they've associated your café with finding me. This isn't good."

"It won't matter, I mean not really." Sandra looked at her like it was obvious. "I mean, because of course I'm coming with you."

"Excuse me?"

"You heard her," Jackson said. "We all are."

Valerie stared at them, totally certain that there was no way that was going to happen. This was going to be too dangerous. It was going to be her against the world, against the three most powerful men in America, for all she knew.

Along the way, she meant to take care of this place that trained assassins. What had the Forsaken called them, back at the Bazaar? The Black Plague, right. She almost laughed, then realized Sandra was frowning.

"Oh, no, I'm not laughing at you all," Valerie said, her smile vanishing. "Just... this is going to be incredibly dangerous, and well..." She glanced over at the three, and could see this was going to be tough. "Jackson, you leave the city and it falls apart. You can't deny it."

"Yeah, but..." He stopped, mouth open, working as he tried to come up with an answer.

He had nothing.

"She has a point there," Sandra said. "But us? We have each other, and that's it."

Sandra wrapped an arm around Diego's waist.

"Exactly my point!" Valerie said, then faked gagging. "You two, can you imagine how going on a trip like this with you would be?"

They looked at her frowning, and Diego said, "Enlighten us, won't you?"

"It'd be sickening! You two are the sappiest love birds I've ever seen, I mean, come on!"

Now it was Jackson's turn to laugh. "She's got that right."

"Shut up," Sandra said to him, then took her arm from around Diego so she could point at Valerie. "And you, get fucking used to it! Because if you think for a second I'm letting you wander off by yourself, with us having no way of knowing how you're doing, or if you'll even make it back, you are sadly delusional."

Valerie pursed her lips, hearing a couple of forks hitting plates in the other room as people reacted to Sandra's yelling. There was once a time when that in itself would have surprised Valerie, back when Sandra was effectively her slave. But now, it had become something of a thing.

"And if you act like this when we're out there?" Valerie said. "When it's life or death on the line, and I tell you to do something, I want to know that you aren't going to turn around and argue with me."

"When?" Sandra beamed. "You did say when, not if."

"Yeah, but I mean—"

"She said 'when'!" Sandra jumped into Diego's arms and they kissed.

"Good luck," Jackson said, stepping up to Valerie. "I'd say it'll be harder to survive these two than anything the CEOs can throw at you."

Valerie ran a hand through her hair and groaned. "You think I really have to take them?"

"No, but… if you're going to, I get dibs on the café. Don't be surprised if all the wine's gone when you get back."

That got Sandra's attention. "Hey, no way. We're already

down because of those stupid pirates. You want me to kick your butt up to Toro or whatever they call that pirate haven up there now?"

"Wait, what?" Jackson glanced around, confused.

"Just, Clive told me about the pirates up there," Valerie said, filling him in. "The ones that almost took us down on the way over here. Apparently, they all have this kind of home base in that area. What used to be Toronto, and it has spread out east. But, wait a sec, Sandra… how do you know about all that?"

Sandra looked to Diego, and he shook his head, just barely. A red aura shot out from them, warm, but not too warm.

"No, no lying," Valerie said, interpreting the sensation. This sort of mind reading was weird, but fairly useful.

Judging by Sandra's annoyed sigh, she didn't seem to think so. "Okay, with all this pirate crap interfering with the business, we've been going down to talk to him recently. Found out a bit more about it, and we're talking about ways to set up a defensive."

"Wait, you're what?"

"You know, like set up a blockade to stop the pirates."

Valerie almost laughed. "Are you saying you've been going behind our backs to try and set up a fleet of ships and airships, basically?"

"More just thinking out loud," Sandra said, clearly affronted. "And just because someone does something without telling you, doesn't mean they're going behind your back."

Valerie frowned, but had to admit that Sandra had a good point. "And you want to put that on hold to wander the wilderness, possibly face nomad tribes and whackos and who knows what else on our way to confront the CEOs in whatever the hell Chicago is like nowadays?"

The question caused Sandra to pause, but then she bit her lip and nodded. "You're my everything, Val. Well, you and Diego here."

Diego took her hand and kissed it.

"Ugh, what did I say about that crap?" Valerie spun around, shaking her head, only to be met by Jackson staring at her with a grin. "Don't you start too now," she said, and then nodded for him to follow. "We can take care of our sappiness in private."

His grin grew even wider, and they headed for the backdoor. It looked like Valerie was taking Sandra and Diego to hunt down the CEOs. In the meantime, they had some preparations to take care of.

Valerie paused and turned back to Sandra. "Let's make sure everything's in place, figure this all out. We have my death to plan, after all."

CHAPTER TWO

Enforcer HQ

Jackson approached Enforcer HQ, moving his neck to work out the kinks after the way Valerie had tossed him around. Damn, he was going to miss her. It was weird knowing that, on the one hand his body was going to go through withdrawal pangs while she was gone, and yet he'd finally have a chance to heal from her wild passion.

He wasn't sure if he should laugh at the way he felt, or cry, at what he was going through physically. Mentally though, he was having a hard time dealing with the fact that she was leaving. Having led his people for so long, he'd come to know loss, and he had definitely learned how to not hold out hope when they went off to accomplish something they needed to do. When that involved revenge, they rarely returned.

Then again, this was Valerie. He had seen firsthand what she was capable of, and had no doubts that it would be incredibly difficult to hurt her, let alone kill her.

But not impossible.

He reached the streets around the building and stopped to stare at the security this place had now. It was no joke. While Strake had ruled with terror, ensuring no one would cause problems because they feared retribution, Colonel Donnoly and the new regime apparently didn't want to take any chances. With the bombings and other attacks that had happened a couple of months back, he couldn't blame them.

The Weres had managed to drag in and set up concrete blocks in staggered positions around the entrance. Also, sniper positions had been set up with sentries, not only on this building, but on several of the surrounding rooftops and in windows overlooking the area.

If anyone tried to rush the building here, they'd be splattered on the ground before stepping two feet. Judging by the reinforced steel and whatnot surrounding the base of the building, explosions wouldn't do much either. Sure, there were still ways he imagined people could cause damage if they set their minds to it, but he was impressed.

"Mercer, my old pal," Dreg, the werebear said, stepping up and looking him up and down. The guy was short but built like a tank with muscles thick as trees. Jackson had heard the whole story of how Valerie met the guy selling blood, so wasn't quite sure how much he liked him or trusted him. The fact that they were giving the guy a job with the cops made him even warier.

So, when Dreg motioned for his weapons, Jackson's first instinct was to hit the guy in the throat. But he had come here with a purpose, so he handed over his pistol and the blade on his belt.

"You have a reason to be here?" Dreg asked.

"Do you?"

Dreg chuckled. "To turn assholes like you around and kick you to the curb."

"Try it. Better yet, hurt me while you're at it, and see if Valerie lets you keep that ugly head of yours."

That sobered Dreg right up, but as he stepped aside and motioned for him to continue on, he mumbled, "Hiding behind your girlfriend will only save you for so long, pal."

"I can hold my own," Jackson said, more to himself, since he was already past, moving for the door.

He went through more rounds of security, saying hello to the various Weres and cops he had come to know over the last couple of months. They trusted him, but still weren't taking any chances. After everything they had been through with Ella and others, everyone had to be checked.

The elevator ride up gave him time to consider how much he was going to miss Valerie. She had grown on him over the last couple of months, as if she had always been part of his life. Now that she was talking about leaving, he would have more time to spend with his people, to tutor Lorain, and to be the leader they needed. No, the leader they deserved.

Times were still tough, what with Morgan still at large. Too many on both sides had been wounded or worse, and he meant to ensure that stopped as soon as Valerie was gone, even if it meant reaching some sort of peace with Morgan.

He reached his floor and found the door shut, so stood outside of Colonel Donnoly's office, waiting patiently and staring at a painting of the fight with Valerie's brother, Donovan. It was dark, with blimps filling the sky, lightning shooting in purple and silver streaks.

The fact that anyone had time to paint for pleasure intrigued him. Then again, there were still the elite of society who seemed to be established enough that they could simply have others working for them, and there were still those who would sponge off their parents, while their parents struggled with two or more jobs.

"You like it?" a voice said, and he turned to see Wallace approaching.

"It's quite well done."

"Thank you," Wallace said. "It's mine."

"As in… you bought it?"

"As in I painted it." Wallace shrugged. "Just something I've been doing between visits with Ella."

"I had no idea you had it in you," Jackson said leaning back to examine the painting. Flawless. "That explains the chaotic feel."

Wallace let out a sorrowful laugh. "It's the only way I've figured out how to cope with all this. I have to believe we can get her back, after she's proven herself."

"Proven herself?" Realization dawned on Jackson. "The raids… she's been giving you all information?"

Wallace nodded. "I hate to use her this way, but… she did betray us, even attacked Valerie in that bar. Why we keep that place open is beyond me—so many problems!"

"Probably because you know Cammie would come in here and bite your head off if you tried to mess with her haunt."

"My man, that lady is scary."

Jackson chuckled, staring back at the painting and getting lost in the small strokes near the bottom, in the dark alleys, which he guessed to be the forces fighting.

"And you?" Wallace stood next to him, also assessing his work. "You seem to be… bothered."

Jackson stared a moment longer, not sure how much he could say about Valerie's decision. They would have to be let in on it, and he came to do just that and more. But how to explain it?

He glanced at the main doors

"Come on," Wallace said, nodding to the doors. "Let's tell the big guy he can't keep you waiting."

Jackson nodded, but paused. "Wallace, more assassins… and this time, one was at the café, waiting. I think we have a mole."

"Damn." Wallace looped his thumbs into his belt, looking in deep thought. "Someone's telling the Forsaken where they can find Valerie?"

"Or where to get to her loved ones, yeah. Can you…?"

"Oh, of course. We'll double up security there, and in the whole area. But, damn." He glanced over to Jackson and his brow furrowed. "Wait, you're not saying, Ella?"

Jackson shook his head. "I have no idea. Does she have outside access?"

"No, and her issue was with allowing vampires to be in charge, not so much a loyalty to the CEOs. In fact, I'm pretty sure she wants to see them go down as much as the rest of us."

"Keep an eye out for anything suspicious from the others then." Jackson nodded to show he was ready, and together they walked to the large oak doors. "If it's one of my people, you might have to arrest me or there's going to be a trail of blood in this city from where I drag this traitor's corpse behind me for all to see."

"Jackson, that's nasty."

Jackson laughed. "We need to show these people that the old days are gone."

Wallace paused, hand on the left door. "By filling them with terror? I'd say rule of law, show them that we're different than the last lot. That we stand with them to see this city safe, not over them."

"And that's why you wear the uniform, isn't it?" Jackson gave a curt nod to show he was done with this conversation, and just then the elevator dinged behind them.

The elevator slid open and then Royland and Cammie entered, sharing a laugh.

"I miss something?" Donnoly's voice came from behind, where Jackson hadn't realized, but the man had opened the door and now stood, waiting.

Cammie glanced between him and the others, and just shrugged. "Nothing that's any of your business."

Royland blushed.

"Well then, if you'd all come in." Donnoly didn't seem to care one bit that Cammie had her little secrets, though it ate at Jackson. Everyone else seemed to be partnering up, based on the look Royland was giving her, while he and Valerie would soon be taking a break. So that she could rush off to arguably the most dangerous situation she had ever found herself in, while many of her allies who had helped her along the way would stay back here, wondering if she was safe.

It would be tough, but it wasn't like he had never dealt with loss and grief. Plus, if anyone could survive, it was Valerie.

They entered and Donnoly took his spot at the head of the table. "Sorry to keep you all waiting. We've just had a raid on one of the underground compounds, and guess what we found?"

"Blood," Royland said, sure of his guess.

Donnoly nodded. "Strake might be gone and the CEOs off doing who knows what, but the blood trade is still alive. Ella might even be able to earn back my trust, if she keeps giving us tips like this one. We might need her out on the streets eventually."

"You can't be serious?" Wallace leaned forward, hands out at his side like he was trying to grasp something. "I mean, I want her to have changed more than any of you, but it's only been a couple of months."

"The need outweighs the risk," Donnoly said. "But the purpose of this meeting," he gestured to Jackson, "why don't you tell us?"

Everyone shifted to look at Jackson, and he paused, trying to think of how to say this. Better out than in, and out as soon as possible. So he just spat it out, "We have to plan Valerie's death."

The entire room held their breaths, staring at him like he was a madman. Wallace's hand started moving slowly for his gun.

And then Jackson realized his mistake.

"Oh, God," he laughed, "no, I don't mean we want to actually kill her. Sorry. I mean she wants to fake her death so she can go after the CEOs without them expecting her. We have to figure out how to make it plausible, realistic. Believable."

"You fucking shit for brains," Cammie said, laughing. "I was about to leap across this table and tear your larynx out."

"Wow, yeah," Donnoly said. "You might want to work on your delivery there. And you," he addressed Cammie, "language here? We're professionals."

She just looked at him like she couldn't tell whether he was serious or not. A sparkle in his eye made Jackson pretty sure he wasn't.

"Again, my mistake." He held up his hands in surrender, figuring he better ease the tension somehow. "Sorry."

They all started laughing, except Cammie who said,

"Wait, leaving? We're going with her, right? I mean, this is the CEOs. She'll need our help."

He shook his head. "I tried that one, but no. She thinks we're all too vital to this city. And let's be clear here, this city needs us. My force needs me, and each of you has a responsibility."

None of them could argue that, nor stand up to Donnoly's look of authority.

Jackson had to admit, Donnoly sure seemed the leader at that moment—maybe Valerie was right, and by the time she left, at least, these folk could be enough for this city to stand on its own. With his help, of course… unfortunately.

"Well now that that's decided," Donnoly turned back to Jackson, "let's plan Valerie's death, shall we?"

They all smiled at that, and leaned forward to start tossing ideas around.

CHAPTER THREE

Black Plague HQ

Robin felt pain coursing through her skull, pounding, throbbing, and then darkness. It was excruciating, nothing like she had ever felt in her miserable sixteen years of life. She curled into a ball on the floor, then turned again with a spasm as the pain reached new heights.

And still she refused to give into it. Somewhere out there, her family was alive, she was sure of it. She couldn't let these bastards win, these men who stood in a circle around her, watching to see what would happen, just watching as she faced the pain.

The tall one, the one they called Giuseppe, had told her that if she could just hold out through the pain, they would let her live. If she didn't, if she gave into it, she would become a mindless slave.

And so she fought, pushing through, nails digging into the floorboards, carving grooves as she screamed out loud.

With one last throbbing pain that left her chest and upper arms twitching, the pain was gone. As it faded, she felt her senses returning, but stronger than ever. Her breathing was heavy as she breathed in the cedar, the aroma of fear-induced sweat from the man they had in the corner, tied and gagged, and, most of all, a scent she had never smelled before but recognized instantly—vampire.

She knew, because she was now one of them.

"Welcome to the Black Plague," Giuseppe said, reaching a hand out to lift her up, staring at her with disbelief.

Her head spun, but it wasn't like she was dizzy. It was like she was experiencing life and balance and true consciousness for the first time ever.

"What have you done to me?" she asked, observing as claws grew from her hands, then retracted.

"Only succeeded in what I have failed at so many times before," Giuseppe said, wrapping an arm around her. She wanted to throw the arm away, or tear it off and beat him with it, but she still wasn't sure how strong she was, and to be honest, these vampires scared the hell out of her. "You're the seventh female we have tried to turn. The first female member of the Black Plague."

She frowned at him, and then at the bound man. "He's next?"

Giuseppe laughed. "He's my supper, after training tomorrow. Well, his blood anyway. You all will get yours, in time."

Her eyes narrowed and she felt a burning rage piling up inside, but for now she swallowed it down. There were too many of his kind here, or, her kind now as well, she supposed. She would fit in with them, figure out what she needed to make it out of here and find out whatever she could about the fate of her family, and then make a break for it.

The days that followed were like nothing she had ever experienced. Growing up in the Fallen Lands, in a small outpost said to have been set up by her father's pastor soon after the days of the collapse and the World's Worst Day Ever, or WWDE, as many referred to it, she had learned how to be a survivor. But here they weren't training to survive, they were training to kill.

It started with a vampire coming around to pound on the doors of the small, one room units the various new vampires were put up in. They had to be outside and ready within two minutes of that knock, and would usually go for a nighttime run.

That first night had ended with them at the bottom of a cliff, where a circle of loose rocks formed perfect fighting pits. While they were still all waking up and settling down from the run, the older vampires gave them knives, taught them a few moves, and then said, "Attack."

"Wait, what?" she said, holding the knife awkwardly and looking back at the vampire. But before he had a chance to answer, her opponent's blade was in her stomach. Fuck, that hurt.

She staggered back, holding the wound. She stared at the young boy who had delivered the blow and was now leering at her like she was his bitch. When she collapsed to the ground and lay back like she was going to die, the closest elder pulled her up by the neck of her shirt, took out the knife, and tossed it to the boy.

"Don't be a drama queen," the elder said, and motioned for them to go at it again.

This time, holding her wound while her mind spun with ideas for how to get out of this, she at least had the smarts to see the attack coming and do something about it. She sidestepped, tripping the boy with her right leg, and then snatched the knife away with a quick twist of his wrist before he hit the ground.

She was more than happy to repay the blow, but hadn't been ready for the scraping on bone she felt as the knife sunk in all the way up to the hilt.

"Who's a bitch now?" she said, and he looked up at her with confusion in his pain-ridden face.

"For the record, I never said that," he replied, then stood. The elder walked past and saw them both bleeding, then shook his head. "Either you're both really good, or really bad at this. Either way, go get rested up, we have target practice next, followed by more hand-to-hand fighting, and I want you two as healed as you can be before that."

When he'd walked off, Robin looked at the boy with a raised eyebrow. "They want us to fight, like this?"

"Feels like you're gonna die, right?" he said, then stuck out a hand. "I'm Brad."

She shook it and forced a smile. The thought of continuing like this made her sick, but when she thought of her family and rescuing them, there wasn't any price too high. So she nodded to the boy, and then they found the area to rest and heal, waiting for the next stage of their training.

A dark object moved in the distance, and when she craned her neck she could see what looked like a black object, large enough to fit several men inside, floating and moving across her line of sight. Moonlight glinted off sleek metal.

"One of the Three Amigos," Brad said.

"What?"

"The ones in charge," the boy said. "I heard some of the elders talking about it yesterday. Apparently, he's making a visit. Making some big plans about some other vampire they're having troubles with. From France or something."

Infighting amongst the vampires? Now that was news.

At that moment, she realized she had forgotten all about the pain. She glanced down and saw that, indeed, the wound had already started to heal. Learning to fight, shoot, and more… and healing when she got stabbed, which they apparently didn't discourage from happening. Life was certainly changing.

A movement caught her eye and suddenly one of the elder vampires sent another one flying back. Instantly he was on him, teeth bared and eyes glowing. He brought down blow after blow on the vampire beneath him, until there wasn't much to be recognized as a face.

Only then did the top vampire stand, look around and say, "He spoke ill of our benefactors, a crime punishable by death. Consider yourselves lucky that you're new recruits to the cause. This guy will heal, the first time."

He walked back over to the group and said, "Back to training!"

Life was changing, and certainly not for the better.

CHAPTER FOUR

Old Manhattan

Valerie loved having Sandra to herself again for the first time in what felt like years. They had found a spot at the outskirts of the main part of the city, on a rooftop where Valerie often found herself lately, attracted by the enticing aroma of the thyme and mint planted there, especially when it wafted along on a cool spring breeze just like today.

"We really have no other options?" Sandra said,

"Not without putting more people at risk." Valerie took a small leaf of mint, crushed it in her fingers, and then breathed in the scent. "I have no tolerance for more innocent death."

"Not that you ever did."

Valerie considered her, head tilted, and said, "Honestly? Toward the end of that Strake business, or even in the Bazaar, I was starting to wonder about it all. Like who had I become? Was this really me?"

"Seriously?" Sandra laughed, leaning over the railing to look out at the debris and ruins in the distance. "I've always loved you, always will. But the Valerie you are now? This woman you've become? That's the real you. That's the Justice Enforcer who will bring the evil of this land to its knees."

"You think?" Valerie joined Sandra against the railing. She was vaguely aware that the metal was cold, but it didn't bother her.

Sandra simply nodded.

"You sure you won't reconsider staying behind?" Valerie asked.

"Do you really want me to?"

"Come on. You know the answer to that as well as I do. No, I love the idea of you coming, but the chance of you being hurt? Or worse? It eats me up at night." She felt the breeze in her hair and closed her eyes, letting the smells of the city flow by, images of people eating in fancy restaurants, others hiding in shadows with drugged out looks in their eyes. "The city still needs a lot of work."

"Which is why you need Jackson here." Sandra laughed. "If you think about it, I should be the fourth amigo, right?"

Valerie turned to her and frowned. "I'm not following."

"You know, the three amigos? The CEOs, and since I've started my own business, you could say I'm one of them."

"You definitely could not. Sandra, I'm pretty sure there are many CEOs in this city still, it just so happens that they called those three *the* CEOs because they were in charge of practically everything in this city."

"Okay, good. But it's a bit… deterring to hear everyone using the term CEO so negatively. I mean, when you see the joy on someone's face when they take a sip of my newest shipment of wine, it's priceless."

"Considering the fact that you're coming with me, I guess that means you just put a price on it."

"That's true. Priceless except when put up against seeing you're safe." Sandra suddenly lit up. "Oh, speaking of the journey, Cammie wanted to take you out for some new outfits before you go. She said you should have traveling clothes, something less conspicuous than tight-ass leather."

Valerie let the purple jacket flow in the wind, so that her tight, leather outfit was visible. "But it looks good, doesn't it? I mean, I'm hot in this thing, and I don't mean in the sweaty way."

"Hot and maybe a bit conceited," Sandra said with a laugh. "But… maybe you should wear a bra under it? You can kinda see your ni—"

"Hey, there's a chill up here," Valerie said, pulling her coat back around her and tying the sash to keep it closed. "Why aren't you coming?"

"I'd go with you, it's just that I have to gather some of the Weres and pick up a new shipment from the docks. Gotta make sure it's right this time, because I'm not paying some captain for goods lost in transit. Not again."

"Pirates?"

"Yeah." A look of annoyance crossed Sandra's face. "I've been talking with Cammie about it, and she's thinking her and Royland can have a little conversation with Clive while I'm gone, you know? Maybe see what he knows about these pirates, then set up a proper defense."

"Right." Valerie nodded, but her mind was on the journey ahead, staring out at the Fallen Lands and wondering what else lay out there.

"Are you even listening to me?" Sandra asked.

"I'm sorry it's just… I get that the café means the world

to you, but it's a little hard for me to spend too much brain power on it when we have people like the CEOs out there and this Black Plague group to deal with."

"Well thank God we're about to take care of them, so we can come back here and finally just settle down and relax."

Valerie stared off, wondering if she could ever really relax, and Sandra shook her head at the look with a "tsk" sound.

"You won't ever be able to just settle down and relax, will you?" Sandra asked.

"In this world?"

She shook her head, then licked her lips as she tried to imagine such a life. Sitting on a couch with Jackson beside her, their small child on her knee, laughing. It sounded great and all, but… maybe not great for her.

"I have this power." Valerie felt herself blush. "I know it sounds stupid, but to have this kind of power and sit back while anyone in the world is suffering just seems so… wrong."

"And if that means we part our ways someday?"

Valerie spun, eyes wide.

"You do realize that has to happen eventually, right?" Sandra looked concerned. "Holy crap, you don't realize that. I mean, Val, that life isn't for me. I'm going to want to settle down someday, have kids, all that stuff."

Valerie was just speechless, then she breathed, trying to keep the anger out of her voice. Anger that her best friend from all these years could even consider abandoning her.

"Then why not start now?" she said. "Why come with me at all?"

Sandra stared off into the distance and shrugged. "One last mission, right? See it through to the end. But then we'll have secured New York, at least from the external threat. We'll still have a lot of work to do here."

"Keeping the law is Donnoly's job now."

"I mean making the city civilized. You can't have a proper city without good wine and cheese."

Valerie laughed at that.

"There's that smile I love," Sandra said, reaching out to place a hand on Valerie's cheek.

Her touch sent a shiver up Valerie's spine, and she reached up and held the hand there, appreciating the warmth of her touch. For a second they were back at that moment, staring out over the fallen Eiffel Tower, when they had kissed.

Part of Valerie wanted that moment back more than anything, but that was the small, incy-wincy part that said a normal life could actually be a reality. That said, Sandra had a point, and that living a life, with a family and all that *normal* stuff, could be in her stars.

She let the hand drop, with a wistful smile.

No, Valerie knew those days were gone, replaced by her role as Justice Enforcer. She had a responsibility to bring judgment, and for reclaiming honor to vampires and the UnknownWorld.

"One last mission, then," Valerie said. "Together, anyway."

Sandra leaned in and kissed Valerie on the cheek, then smiled with a fire in her eyes. "Let's make it count. I want the world quivering in their boots when they think about messing with us."

Valerie laughed. "Damn straight."

They headed out to meet Cammie, and said their goodbyes, and soon Valerie and Cammie were walking along Capital Square, selecting outfits and having a great time. The key was to wear something that wouldn't make her stand out if she needed to stop by other cities along the way, and that hid who she really was when it came time to leave.

As the day wore on and then evening approached, the two sat on one of the benches lining the square, watching people pass by. Valerie had a new sweater on, along with sunglasses and a red hat. Totally not her style, but that was why she figured it would help keep people from noticing her.

"You ever wonder if you could've played your cards differently when you first arrived?" Cammie asked. "I mean, was there a scenario where everyone fell in love with you like we have, and it all just worked out perfectly?"

Valerie laughed at the thought. "You know, I doubt it. Maybe if I'd stayed in the shadows from the get go and gotten to know the various faction leaders, then worked with Jackson to put all of the right pieces in order… but then who knows how many others might have died. How many vampires would have suffered during that time, and how many of ol' Strake's Enforcers would have been able to wander these streets doing whatever the hell they wanted?"

Cammie nodded. "Yeah, that's what I was thinking. You get the lesser of two evils, if you're lucky."

"Right, like you and Royland," Valerie said with a wink.

"We're not a thing," Cammie said, frowning.

"Tell him that, with the way you've been flirting with him and leading him on."

"Well, there was almost that time, and … oh come on, why am I telling you this?"

Valerie scoffed. "Let's see, maybe because we're two grown women who just bonded over a shopping trip?"

Cammie laughed. "Yeah, I feel like we should be gossiping about our friends while eating cookies and sipping tea. I mean, the two of us shopping as if there wasn't anything more important in the world."

"Hey, I had a damn good time." Valerie stared waiting.

"You're not off the hook that easily."

Cammie rolled her eyes. "Would I like to see what he's working with? Yeah, of course. Dude's sexy as hell, for a vampire. No offense."

Valerie frowned. "Romance between a vampire and a Were, I could see how that would get tricky."

"Really?"

"No, not at all. I'm giving you a hard time for being a racist, or speciesist, or whatever the term is for what we are. You're telling me that if I were a man, you wouldn't hit this because I'm a vampire?"

"You'd be sexy as hell as a man, let's just get that on the table." Cammie let a small laugh escape, then looked Valerie up and down like she was about to jump her bones. "Yep, I'd totally do you if you were a dude. Vampire or not."

Valerie wasn't sure how to feel about this conversation, but she had been largely responsible for starting it, so she simply smiled. "Thank you. So the problem is... Royland's not hot enough? I doubt that, because I've seen him, and I gotta say..."

"Smoking, yes, I agree." Cammie stared off into the distance considering, then frowned. "I don't know. Relationships, ever since my days out in the Fallen Lands and then in the Golden City, there's something not right," she knocked on her head, gently, "up here. I mean, I flirt like crazy, and maybe someday it'll be different. But right now the idea of allowing him in terrifies the hell out of me."

"Letting him in... your heart?"

"What else... oh, God." Cammie laughed. "Yeah, the idea of letting him in somewhere else does the opposite of terrify me, that's for damn sure."

Valerie chuckled. "Okay, well, give it time. You never

know, and in conditions like these, you never know how long each of you has anyway."

"Wow, talk about a downer," Cammie said, standing and grabbing the bags. "Come on, I want to show you something before everyone starts showing up." Cammie stood to go. Her face scrunched as she realized she might have said something she didn't mean to. "Er, that is…"

"Show up to what?" Valerie asked, even more curious following Cammie's reaction. "Wait a minute… that's why she wanted you to take me shopping!"

"No, stop thinking," Cammie said.

"She's putting together some sort of surprise for me? A surprise going away party?"

"What? No, I never said that."

"Ooh, this is exciting," Valerie said, ignoring Cammie's lame attempts at denying it. "I mean, she's coming too, so it's kind of a surprise party for herself too, but she's throwing it, so that's a bit weird, but okay. This is going to be fun!"

Cammie just shook her head. "Don't tell her I let it slip, please … and act surprised."

"You got it. Now, what was this that you wanted to show me?"

Cammie's smile returned, eyes sparkling. "Come on, I think it could be huge."

"We aren't still talking about Royland, right?"

Cammie hit her playfully, and they laughed as she led them to whatever this special something was.

CHAPTER FIVE

Black Plague HQ

Robin was starting to get the hang of this lifestyle. Running two to three times a night, training with swords, knives, and guns, and even learning about the various poisons available to them.

On her third night of training she and the others were told to line up in the courtyard of their headquarters—an old stadium, converted for this purpose. They stood at attention as three vampires marched out before them, clad all in black from head to toe, including masks on their faces, rifles slung over their backs, swords on their hips, and pistols strapped to their thighs. It was almost comical, Robin thought, if it weren't for the potential death and destruction these three could cause.

A flash of terror caused her heartbeat to increase and she felt it pulsing in her fingertips. One of them looked her way with thin, almost black eyes, and she realized why that emotion had hit her—that man had been there when her settlement had been attacked.

He had been one of several to help drag her off, kicking and screaming.

For all she knew, he had killed her parents.

But no, she wouldn't accept that. She couldn't think for a second that they were dead or this would all be pointless. Better to throw herself on her own sword now, if that were the case.

That, or see that this man and every other one of these bastards suffered worse fates than even she could possibly fathom. Oh, but she would come up with something.

"Psst," Brad whispered at her side.

She started, catching herself before looking over. "What?" she whispered.

"Keep it down."

"Keep what down?"

"You were breathing super loud, like you're about to hyperventilate or something."

Before she could respond, Giuseppe stepped in front of them all, clad all in black as well, minus the facemask. He faced the three and crossed his arms before him in salute. The three did the salute back, and then turned and strode off past the courtyard gates.

Giuseppe turned back to the recruits and smiled. "Each of you will be put to good use, soon enough. They will kill the one known as Valerie, and come back with her head, or we'll have each of theirs."

"Is this all we train for?" a man near the front said. "Just let me after her."

Giuseppe laughed, then said, "Good, you're next. But no, we have our orders in the meantime, and soon you will be put to the test. A large city nearby is already being scouted, and we mean to make it ours. It's rife with opportunity and fresh recruits."

"Chicago?" Brad whispered, but Robin shrugged. She knew it wasn't far, but had heard stories about the people who ran the city. About a group called the FDG, or Force de Guerre. If they were going up against the FDG, they had damn well better be sure they were as trained as they could be.

"Carry on," Giuseppe shouted, waving them off. "Train your hardest, or you will fall when it's your time. If you let that happen, I can guarantee you I'll be coming after you in hell to kick your ass as many times as I can until my leg tires. Just remember that."

Brad stifled a laugh, but Robin shot him a glare.

He shrugged, and nodded for her to follow. "Come on, let's see what you're made of."

She looked around, confused.

"Free training," he said leading her to one of the main training pits set up at the edges of the courtyard. "You can do weapons, obstacle courses, your choice. Thought maybe I'd give you some pointers on ground combat."

"Is that right?" she asked, amused.

He winked, and then charged. Without a second thought, she had stepped around him and brought her hand down to slap him on the rear. They both froze and he looked at her with a bit of hurt pride, a bit of interest.

"Did you just… slap me?"

"Shut up and try again." She couldn't help but smile, biting her lip to try and hide it. The act didn't help though, unless her goal had been to offend him.

This time he came in low and got her before she had a

chance to react, lifting her by the legs and slamming her onto the ground. As quick as she could blink, he had shuffle-stepped around her and was on top of her, wrapping an arm around her neck.

She thrust up with her hips and twisted, managing to get herself in an awkward position between his legs with one arm trapped up by her head, the other below.

"Spank me again," he said, "see what happens."

"Get off!" she grunted, trying to twist again.

He laughed again and said, "Sure," before snatching her arm and throwing a leg over her head to put her in an arm bar.

"Let go, you dick!" she shouted, but he just pulled harder.

"No, you have to get out of it. You have to learn!"

She shouted in pain, and then struggled, so he pulled harder.

"Push through the pain," he said, and then thrust his body back so that her arm cracked with a shooting pain.

Screw this, she thought, eyes watering. She brought her leg up to kick him in the face, then twisted, breaking free from the hold so that her butt was in his face, his crotch exposed.

"Training, training!" he said.

But she was pissed.

"Push through the pain," she said, and brought her hand down like a hammer on his nuts.

"FUCK!" he said, pushing her off so that she went sprawling in the dirt.

Holding her damaged arm, she quickly recovered and spun to see if he was about to attack again.

Giuseppe winked from where he was watching a couple of others train, and then shouted over, "You'll both heal. Get over it and get back to training."

"She hit me in the balls!" Brad whined.

Giuseppe looked at him thoughtfully, tilted his head, and said, "Hmm, that's never happened to me. Weird. Let me know if that doesn't heal. Maybe she's just discovered the male vampire's one true weakness."

Several others in the area burst into laughter, and Brad's face went red as he lay there, glaring at her.

The laughter and smiles her way made her beam, at least until she saw the look of betrayal in Brad's face.

He had nearly broken her arm, right? Was she really supposed to sit there and let him abuse her while she did nothing? No way, they were training to fight, to kill even, so if he had to hold his crotch for a couple of minutes and whine like a little babe, then, oh well.

Still, she felt a little bad, and decided to offer him a hand up.

"You have to admit, you were being a bit of a dick." She stood over him, hand held out for truce. "But, if it helps, I feel slightly bad about your family jewels."

He glared, but after a moment he breathed out and took the hand, lifting himself to stand.

"Back to training?" she asked.

"Yeah, but… give me a few minutes. And maybe we take it a little easy on each other."

"Screw that," she said. "This is too much fun. I bet I only got one of them last time, I want to make it an even pair."

"Not. Funny. At. All."

"Okay, okay." She laughed. "No nut shots if you don't try to break any limbs."

He nodded. "Deal."

They got back into it, sparring, blocking, and even getting

a bit into sword fighting. By dark, they had trained their hearts out and their swords were full of chips in the steel. The trainers brought them to a grassy bank along a river, where they were given sharpening stones, then set to sharpening and cleaning their blades.

She saw Brad nearby, shifting uncomfortably where he sat. A couple of the other boys and men adjusted in their seats when she glanced their way as well. Great, she'd suddenly become the girl everyone associated with pain in the crotch.

Maybe that was a good thing, she thought. It would help keep them off of her, at any rate. Not that any of them had tried anything, but she imagined that, when living with a bunch of vampires who had attacked her people and dragged her off, not many of them had strong moral lines that they wouldn't cross.

Giuseppe walked past, then saw her looking, and nodded. When she didn't look away, he walked over.

"Is something bothering you, little birdy?"

"Little birdy?" she asked, confused by that.

"I see that look in your eyes, there's no hiding it from me. That desire to fly away. Well if that's it—"

"No. I mean, no, sir. It's just that… why aren't there more girls?"

"The elusive female vampire," he said with a knowing look. "Haven't I told you that you were the seventh attempt? The others all lost it, went mad."

"But you kept trying. Why?"

He shrugged. "My thoughts are my own, but I'll tell you this—the vampire we mean to kill is a female, and it would be a shame to take one out of this world without first putting another in her place."

"The one they call Valerie?"

He nodded and sat down beside her. "They say she's ruthless, without shame when it comes to taking a vampire's life. Or a human's for that matter. Anyone who stands in her way, who even thinks about questioning this so-called justice of hers. Should anyone like that be allowed to continue on?"

She shook her head.

"Exactly." He put a hand on her shoulder and, for a moment, she felt a rush of terror and panic as she thought he was going to kiss her, but he smiled and simply used her shoulder to push himself up. "Remember, everyone believes they're the hero of their own story, so… be wary of what you hear about her. Let the deaths of those hundreds of vampires she's slain speak louder than rumors."

As he walked off, Robin noticed Brad glancing over from where he knelt, cleaning his own sword.

"Think it's true?" she asked.

"What's true?" he asked, glaring.

"I mean, what he's saying. Maybe we're really here fighting for our world, not trying to hurt people, but to stop this other vampire from her evil ways?"

"You think I'm a bad guy?" he asked. "Oh yeah, I guess you do. Wouldn't have slammed me in the nuts otherwise."

"Come on, you were trying to break my arm."

"No, I was helping you. Damn. I mean, maybe I got carried away, but I didn't ground-pound you in the snatch or anything like that."

"Wow," she said, rolling her eyes. After a minute of cleaning her sword, she glanced back over to see him staring at her, a look of confusion on his eyes. "What?"

"You really thought I was trying to hurt you?"

"I thought you were being a dick."

He set the sword aside and stood, walking over with his

hand held out. "Peace?"

She smirked. "Yeah, okay. I mean, I did feel bad. Are they…?"

He pulled back, and then laughed. "You don't really ask if that area's okay after what you did. I mean, it's kind of weird. Let's just say that, yes, I'm healed."

"Good, I'd hate to have you running into war, wobbling the whole time because you couldn't walk straight or something."

"We just made a truce," he said. "Probably not the time to crack jokes about my nether regions."

"Right, sorry."

Suddenly his face went pale and he was back at his sword, pretending like they hadn't been speaking at all. She looked around, confused, and then saw why.

That black, floating vehicle was back, and a large man with silvery wisps of hair had just exited with three vampires at his side.

They seemed to be looking over the vampires in training. The assassins.

"Giuseppe," one of the vampires called out, and Giuseppe double-timed it over to them. "The move on Chicago, how're we looking?"

It was hard to hear Giuseppe's response from this far away, but Robin was pretty sure he had said they were on track.

The rest of the conversation she missed, because they had turned and were walking the other way as they spoke.

The look on Brad's face said exactly what she was feeling though—they were expected to make a raid on a major city, defended by, if the rumors around here were true, Weres.

While the training was going well, she didn't feel anywhere near ready for something like that.

CHAPTER SIX

Below Old Manhattan

"Sandra's going to be pissed if we show up smelling like sewage," Valerie said, working her way along the sewage walkways, Cammie in the lead.

"Would someone have set up traps like I'm telling you about if they weren't protecting something insanely valuable?" Cammie paused, checking her directions, and then pointed, paused, and pointed the other way. "Over here, yeah, definitely."

"Okay, just remember, she did all this for me, and I'm not supposed to know. If I show up late, or let on that I know, she's going to freak. And if that happens, I'm putting all that woman's frustration and anger your way."

"I'm pretty sure I can handle it," Cammie said with a scoff.

"Then you're an idiot."

Cammie paused to look back and frown. "You're not the only one with people waiting, you know that? Yeah, that's right, I know Jackson wants to see you there."

Valerie felt a heaviness in her heart at the mention of Jackson. In spite of everything else now being taken care of, her relationship, if you could call it that, was the one thing she wasn't sure of. Not wanting to focus on that, she asked, "What's up with you and Royland then?"

"You asking if he was good in the sack? Let me just put it this way, the man can stay up all night."

"Yes, he *is* a vampire, after all." Valerie chuckled. "But no, I wasn't asking about that at all."

"Oh, his size, it's—"

"No, la-la-la-la," Valerie stuck her fingers in her ears and gave Cammie a look. When it was safe, she stopped and said, "Can you please? I don't want to think about my friends that way."

Cammie just looked at her and shook her head, then made a gesture with two hands that Valerie not only didn't understand, but was now stuck with an even worse image of Cammie and Royland together.

"Thanks," Valerie said, sarcasm heavy in her voice. "I really needed that."

"Ah, you and Jackson aren't doing so well?" A look from Valerie and Cammie caught herself. "If not that, is it his..." She glanced down at her hands, still held apart, "Ohhh, sorry."

"No, dammit, there's nothing wrong with—"

"Oh, great!" Cammie perked up, looking past Valerie. "Here it is."

Valerie breathed deep, telling herself to calm the hell down. She stepped up beside Cammie to see where the walkway gave out to a rock surface that led back into a bit of a cave. Sure enough, with her ability to see in the dark she saw hints of the traps, and her curiosity was piqued.

The first step nearly took off Valerie's leg, but she was quick enough to dodge. Then came a slicing blade, and hell, she needed that haircut anyway, even if the result was a bit lopsided.

"Someone's definitely twisted to have set all this up," Valerie said after they had finally passed by a handful of them, and then there was a wall that she realized could be pulled, but when she tried, it was clearly nearly impossible.

Well, nearly impossible. She put everything she had into it, shouting with the effort and feeling her muscles being pushed to the point of breaking, and then, to the surprise of both of them, it moved and revealed a passageway.

"Holy crap," Valerie said. "We did it."

"Holy shit-sticks, you're right." Cammie smirked. "Told you we'd find something."

They moved along the passageway until they came out in a large room with bamboo floors. Cammie coughed, likely due to the air and dust from the crap way they came in. She hit a light switch, and the lights buzzed on.

It wasn't your typical underground hideout. In fact, the place was massive. Continuing the exploration, all Valerie could think was that whoever had lived here must have been incredibly wealthy to put all this together, and they must have done it a long time ago. The initial room they found had to be at least twelve-hundred square feet, and as they explored more, they discovered there were a total of five bedrooms, three floors, and it was complete with a kitchen, bathroom, and more. Valerie was surprised to see there was even a television (though she only recognized it from old pictures), and a *lot* of books.

The books part of it made her wonder. Such a collection

didn't seem like a Forsaken thing to have, and the CEOs never would have been strong enough to enter through the way they had come in.

"Wait a minute," Valerie said, looking over to see a knowing look on Cammie's face.

"I think so too," Cammie said. "When I found it, I was certain it had to be someone like him, right? Because who else but you and him could get that door open. I couldn't even get it to budge, and I'm at least as strong as most vampires. Then when we walked in here, I was certain it was—"

"Michael's," they both said together.

"Wow," Valerie said.

"Holy shitsticks is what I think you were going for there. Or maybe son-of-BITCHquick pancake."

Valerie shot her a frown, wondering what had gotten her all weirded out, and then remembered how, when they had first met, Cammie had been obsessed with the idea of Bethany Anne. She'd even knelt and thought that maybe Valerie could be The Queen Bitch herself, returned.

Being this close to the man who had something to do with her creation must feel like a priest discovering the actual crucifixion cross, or something similar. Okay, that was a horrible simile, she decided, but she had to admit, her head was swimming a bit too much with the excitement of finding this place.

Was it truly possible that Michael could have set this place up years ago, before the great collapse even? Had he visited while in the city, before showing up for the fight between her and her brother, Donovan?

She turned to see that Cammie had wandered off while she was thinking, and so called out, "Cammie?"

"Come see what I found!"

Valerie frowned and descended some stairs until she was on the bottom floor, where there was a large vault door as tall as her head.

"You know what this is, right?" Cammie said, looking at her with excitement practically pouring out of her.

"What?"

"All of his treasure, right? I mean, what else would he keep in here?"

"Cammie, he wasn't some dragon who horded treasure or whatever you seem to be thinking right now."

"I know that," she said, frowning. "But he must've had something after all that time. Something super valuable that's locked up behind these doors right now… waiting… for us."

"If there is, and he didn't take it…"

"Then he'd be fine with us checking." Cammie smiled and turned the handle. Nothing. "I mean, I didn't expect it to just open, but thought it was worth a shot."

Valerie approached the keypad on the front of the massive, black, iron door. She considered for a moment, and then said, "Maybe we can guess his password? I'll try Bethany Anne." She did, but it didn't work. She pursed her lips and tried her second guess, saying, "Michael." Nothing. "Dammit!" She spit out, frustrated. Her voice started as a whisper, "You fucking DOOR!" She yelled, "Give me a damned clue!"

Valerie started looking around for something metal. At least she could vent a little frustration. Although, beating the crap out of Michael's door might not be considered very polite.

She turned to look at Cammie when an electronic voice responded, "Door is listening."

Both woman turned to look at the doors, their eyes wide open.

"Go ahead!" Cammie whispered, "Tell it something!"

Valerie slapped Cammie's hand away from her arm, "Like what?"

"Open sesame?" Cammie asked, looking at Valerie, her eyes afire.

It was all Valerie could do to not roll her eyes, but she called out, "Door, Open Sesame."

"Incorrect request," the electronic voice came back.

Cammie shrugged when Valerie turned back to stare at her, "Any other bright ideas?"

An hour later, Valerie was wishing she had never asked the werewolf Alpha for ideas.

Valerie stared at the door for a moment and then walked up and rubbed a hand across it, wondering aloud. "What are you?"

"I am an arms locker." Came back the electronic voice.

"You have got to be kidding me!" Cammie whispered, annoyance plain in her voice from behind Valerie, "All you have to do is ask it questions?"

Valerie shrugged, "Beats me." She replied. "Arms Locker, what can you do?"

"Open, shut, lock, release," came back a litany of commands, "All other commands are reserved."

"Wonder what those are?" Cammie asked before Valerie looked over her shoulder, annoyed. Cammie put up her hands in defense, "Hey! Just curious."

Valerie shook her head, "Open up."

Nothing happened.

"Open up arms locker."

"Permission from?"

Now, Valerie was on firmer footing, "Michael."

"Incorrect name." The door replied. Valerie heard a snort behind her.

"Open up arms locker, Permission provided by Michael Nacht."

"Code Word?" Asked the Arms locker and Valerie tried 'Michael.'

Nothing happened.

"Yeah, well, what kind of guy uses his own name as a password?" Cammie scratched her chin, but then her eyes went wide. "What if—"

"Not his name, but the meaning of his name!" Valerie interrupted.

"Oh, interesting, yeah try that."

"What?" Valerie stared, waiting. "What were you going to say?"

"Nothing, I'm just—getting hungry I think. I was going to say his favorite food."

Valerie looked back at her friend, "Do you even know his favorite food?"

Cammie pursed her lips in thought. "Um, blood?"

"Wow." Valerie shook her head. "Just… wow. That's so something like racist."

"Okay, smarty-pants, what does his name mean?"

For a moment, Valerie stared at the safe, thinking back to that moment on the blimp when she had first seen Michael, and the thrill that seeing him had sent through her bones. He was all powerful, he was their Dark Messiah, returned.

"Not means, but where did the name come from?" Valerie said, reaching up so that her fingers rested on the door. "This old priest back in France, used to talk about the apocalypse mostly, but sometimes he'd rage about the days of the devil being thrown out from the heavens, and he mentioned a sort of right hand of God, Michael, an *Archangel.*"

She cleared her throat, "Open up Arms Locker, permission

granted by Michael Nacht, code word ArchAngel."

As she said it, something within the door whirred. Then, with a click, the door inched open. She had to use her strength to move the thick iron the rest of the way. They walked through the door into the small room where armor and swords and knives were all stored, in immaculate condition. Then she stared in awe. A pristine set of armor hung as if for decoration, as new and clean as if it had been hung there yesterday.

"His armor," Cammie said, staring in awe.

The two stood there for a minute, then Valerie turned to take in the underground house. This had been Michael's hideout in the city, where he lived and trained. Standing here, knowing that he was off doing his part to bring honor to the vampires, and she was here serving that purpose in America, well, it meant the world to her.

And now they had his armor too.

It was as if she could feel Michael and Bethany Anne there with them, smiling, maybe giving them a nod of approval.

With a smile, Valerie said, "Okay, we can come back later. But let's not make them wait any more for us."

Cammie had her hand gently touching a wall, as if she didn't believe it was there, but then snapped out of it and nodded. "Agreed."

They walked back in silence, both in awe of what they'd discovered. Before leaving, the two paused to close the door and reset the traps, so this place could be properly preserved until Michael's return. Their little secret.

◈ ◈ ◈

Sandra wanted everything to be perfect for the surprise party. She had arranged her best wine, one that dated back to the first post-collapse, from the vineyards of France, or at least so the captain who had sold it to her claimed.

Cheese was spread out with freshly baked bread, along with special meats she had imported as well. It wasn't as much as she would have liked, given the interruptions to the imports from overseas. If Cammie and Royland really could come up with a way of dealing with them before she came back, she would be ecstatic.

If not, she was going to seriously consider bringing the wine making here. Cheese would be tough, as everything they got now was from farms in Portugal and Spain, if the captains were to be believed. Sometimes she thought they were just saying it to make the goods sound more exotic.

Either way, she hadn't noticed any farms near Old Manhattan, that was for sure. Grapes could grow in limited supply, but that wouldn't do to meet the demand she was already faced with.

Even in this torn up world, New Yorkers loved whatever bits of decadence they could get.

"Need help with anything?" Diego asked, stepping up behind her and wrapping his arms around her, then purring seductively in her ear.

"Yeah, I need help controlling my boyfriend," she replied. "He seems distracted."

He pulled back and leaned against a wooden chopping block. "Everyone's ready. She late?"

Sandra frowned, too worried about getting everything perfect to even think about what time it was.

"Now that you mention it."

"Wait…" His ears perked and he smiled. "Come on."

"Wait, the trays!" she said as she went back for the cheese and nodded for him to grab some wine.

They carried them out through the curtains, and then joined the other cops, Weres, and vampires. Curtains covered the windows and glass door, with a sign that said closed on the outside.

Cammie was supposed to bring Valerie back here to show Sandra her new outfits, and that was when the surprise would come.

"I think you should show her the green top first," Cammie's voice said, muffled from the back room along with the sound of two people entering.

"Sandra's never really liked me in green…"

"SURPRISE!" everyone shouted as the two walked in under the curtain.

"And I love you in green," Sandra said, to a room full of laughter. "It's blue I never liked. Too depressing."

"But I almost always wear blue!" Valerie protested, hands on her hips as she looked around the room, taking everyone in. "This is too much, guys!"

Sandra beamed, but then noticed the slightly guilty look on Cammie's face. Using the excuse of handing out cheese while Valerie took turns saying 'hi' to everyone, Sandra whispered to Cammie, "You let it slip."

Cammie pursed her lips. "Maybe a little."

"One thing I ask—"

"Hey, I'm a werewolf, not a damned safe deposit box. You want secrets, don't come to me."

"Strange," Sandra said, eyes narrowed, "how yesterday I distinctly remember you saying something along the lines of Weres being the best secret holders."

"We're also great at adapting to our surroundings, and

right now, my surroundings include people looking to drink and be merry. So…" She gave Sandra a shrug and quickly side-stepped out, then maneuvered to the other side of the room.

Oh well, no use being upset when it was already done. Valerie did seem pleased, regardless of how surprised she was.

Sandra scrunched her nose at a lingering scent that seemed to have come from Cammie, but then it was gone. Like stale water, or rotten eggs.

All of the guests were trying to get their time with Valerie, though they hadn't all been told the specifics. Just that the three would be going on a trip. Those that were in the know, like Wallace, knew to keep their mouths shut, while others had stayed at Enforcer HQ to keep up the defenses, or patrol the streets. Security had been doubled around the square and within a one-mile radius of the café.

That didn't stop Sandra from glancing around with worry. Passersby were bound to hear all the chatter, and maybe catch a glimpse of light past the curtains. Private parties were incredibly rare around here, so she told herself the extra attention was nothing to worry about.

"This is some get together you've put on here," Royland said, and she turned to see him sipping on a glass of red—the merlot, she guessed, knowing his tastes. "If we got hit right now, this city would be doomed."

"You have people on the lookout?"

He nodded.

"Then I'm not too worried."

They both turned to watch Valerie working the crowd, laughing and slapping shoulders.

"It's fake, you know," Sandra said. At a glance from him

she added, "All of that, it's not her. She has always been better off by herself, or with one or two good friends. I think it's why she tried going into the shadows, before. She learned that it's good to have others nearby who you can rely on, but I think she'd be happiest out there kicking bad guys in their throats."

Royland chuckled and massaged his throat. "I'm certainly glad I'm on the right side then."

"That's right, you weren't always, huh?"

"Not exactly, no. Depending on how you define good and bad. Was I striving for a higher place? No. In fact, I cared only for survival. Survival of my people, and to achieve that I allowed the unthinkable to happen."

He looked troubled, a darkness taking over his eyes, so she put a hand on his arm and said, "Your past isn't important here. We've all done bad things to save those we love."

"Maybe."

She stared at him a moment longer, wondering if he was going to tell her what was bothering him, but then Cammie came by, wearing her cowboy boots and a broad smile, and swept him away.

The man had some secrets, maybe a dark side to him still, Sandra thought.

An opening finally came and Sandra squeezed in. She didn't want to occupy Valerie's time, but just give her a hug and say, "Happy going away!"

Valerie laughed. "You're coming with me."

"I know… but I wanted to make sure you understood how much everyone here loves you. For some reason, I get the feeling you don't see this place as home quite like I do."

"Could it be because, until recently, they hunted vampires for their blood?" Valerie whispered. "Or maybe the fact that half the city still seems to want me dead… that might be it."

"But… friends." Even as Sandra said it, she understood Valerie's point. It was hard to feel you belong even when a few people really want you there. It had been that way for her among the vampires under The Duke, when most vampires saw her as food or fuel for the next mission, and only Valerie truly treated her as a friend, albeit like a slave at times.

Valerie saw the look in her eyes, and Sandra knew the woman was doing that mind-reading thing, or whatever it was she sometimes did. It kinda creeped her out, but she smiled, trying to convey joy and excitement.

With a laugh, Valerie said, "Even without my weird creepy powers, I know you better than that."

Sandra blushed and gave her a friendly push. "Go play with your friends, I've got to open another bottle the way Royland's drinking."

Before Sandra could go, Valerie grabbed her arm. "Thank you, I mean it."

She nodded, and this time the smile was genuine.

As Sandra retreated to the kitchen, she gave Diego a wink and noticed the heavy way his eyes moved over her. Great, he was already a bit tipsy. Normally she wouldn't mind, especially since he got a bit handsy when he had something to drink, and she liked the extra attention. But she had hoped he would help her clean this place up tonight.

Oh well, there was always tomorrow… or maybe she could pay someone else to do it.

At the curtains, Presley stumbled into her path, then paused and looked up at her with wide, captivating eyes.

"What's she see in you?"

"Excuse me?" Sandra asked.

"This vampire lady, what's she always keeping you around for?"

Sandra frowned. Was this Were for real?

"Can't you see," Esmerelda said, stepping up behind Sandra. She lifted Sandra's wrist, where scar marks from teeth still remained, though faint. "This one's just food." She leaned in and sniffed, then added, "I sure would like a taste."

"Since I'm not sure if you're hitting on me or threatening me," Sandra said as she pulled away, "let's just call it neither and say I got something to do."

Esmerelda shrugged and put her arm around Presley, so that the two watched Sandra as she ducked into the back room.

Maybe she wouldn't miss this city as much as she had been starting to think. No, this was her new home. The city where she and Diego had come together, and it would always hold that for her. As soon as this mission was over, she'd be right back with him.

She found one of the less special bottles, figuring the taste wasn't as important the more bottles they all drank, and was winding the cork when the first gun shots sounded.

Pausing, counting her heart beats, she listened, taking a moment to process the fact that they weren't nearby.

Two sniper shots sounded in response, and then more shooting and a distant shout.

She ran back into the main room and everyone was murmuring, a couple moving for the door.

"The back!" Valerie hissed, stepping up to redirect them past Sandra.

Sandra spun, looking for Diego, but saw him slipping out through the crowd. That drunken idiot.

"Val!" she called, and nodded for the door. "Watch out for him?"

Valerie smiled and winked, then reached for her hip—only, her sword wasn't there. She must have left it behind when she went shopping, Sandra realized.

"I put it in the cupboard!"

Valerie said, "Thanks!" And ran off to join the rest. Most of the guests lingered, including Lorain and Jackson, the latter of whom was more focused on the cheese. He saw her looking and shrugged.

"Another night in the good ol' NYC," he said, and raised his cup.

"I'm not cheering that," she replied, and then started cleaning up the place.

◈ ◈ ◈

Capital Square Side Streets

Diego was about sick of this shit. He had been sitting there, enjoying the nice evening his girl had put together, and then some asshole comes along and interrupts it with a gunfight?

No way.

He charged out, making a semi-drunk decision to remember not to transform out in public and scare off half the citizens.

Suddenly two wolves tore past him, and he frowned, turning back to see Cammie running up behind him.

"They're with me," she said. "Don't worry about it. Which way?"

As if in answer, another gun shot rang out, not far to their left. They all diverted that way, and came out just as Peterson turned toward them, rifle aimed directly at them. They froze, and for a long moment, they all stared.

Finally, Wallace stepped forward and Peterson showed recognition, lowering the rifle.

"What happened?" Wallace asked, gesturing to the bodies farther down the alley.

"More of them," Peterson said. "Morgan's people tried to make a move. Good thing we were here."

Cammie and the two wolves went charging on ahead, not replying when he called after them that he thought that was the last of it.

"Better to make sure," Diego said. He blinked, hard, realizing just how tipsy he was.

"Where've you been, anyway?" Wallace asked his old partner. "Donnoly really has you on patrol tonight?"

"Security for your little get together, actually."

Diego stumbled and steadied himself against the nearby brick wall, then saw Valerie perched on the two-story building nearby, glancing around, then staring down at him.

This couldn't be it, could it? Was this the moment? A crowd was gathering along the square, and she was walking toward them at the edge of the roof.

On the street below, Jackson came out of a nearby alley, a gang of men and women following, many armed.

Holy shit, this was it, and he had been stupid enough to think it wouldn't happen until he was ready.

"Where's that murderous bitch at?" Jackson called out, loud enough for everyone in the square to hear.

This was either it, or Jackson had just switched sides. Dammit, Diego wished he had stopped at the first glass of wine. His head was spinning and he wasn't thinking straight. He being a Were, it would clear up fast, but in the meantime he chided himself for over indulging.

Suddenly, everyone was pointing to a lit-up spot near

the center of the square but off to the side, where the crowd couldn't quite reach her.

"We knew you were still around," Jackson said, stepping into the square. The crowds that remained after the gunfire from moments before stepped aside, making room, already scared, though not scared enough to miss whatever this was.

Diego stepped forward too, cautious, eyes darting between Valerie, Jackson, and the café where he hoped Sandra had stayed out of sight.

"What is this?" Valerie called down to Jackson. "I own this city now. It was I who took down the faction leaders, I who killed Commander Strake!"

"And it is I who will unite this city once and for all," Jackson said, and he ran for her, guns drawn, shooting.

The crowd screamed, backing up farther now, but there were a couple who Diego noticed didn't bother to move but just watched. One, a woman with red hair—Morgan.

Diego considered running forward and breaking it up, but there was something about the way those two were shouting at each other that, even in his inebriated state, sounded way too corny.

Holy crap, he thought for the millionth time. This was it.

And then they were wrapped in combat, arms flailing, shots fired, and then, right before everyone's eyes, Valerie fell.

Only, the shot wasn't from Jackson, nor any of his companions, which seemed contrary to the point in Diego's opinion.

He frowned, joining the rest in looking for the shooter, and then he saw the dark form on a nearby roof, taking aim again. He was going for Jackson this time.

Diego was on it, charging as he shouted, "Get down!" and then snatched a rifle from one of Jackson's people and was shooting at the figure.

A curse sounded and then another one appeared, sword slashing at Diego. More screams and more gunshots, as the crowd pushed back farther.

Get out of here! Diego thought as he defended strike after strike. This guy was fast—dressed in black from head to toe, pistols on his hips and coming at him with two long blades.

There was no way around it. If Diego hoped to stand a chance, he had to transform, right here, in front of everyone.

It was keep the secret, or his life. He chose his life.

Gasps filled the square as he transformed, and a moment later, no longer held back by inhibitions of keeping the UnknownWorld secret, since Diego had ruined it, more people were transforming. Two werewolves came to his aid, and a couple of vampires were shimmying their way up the side of the building to get to the shooter, who aimed in at Valerie again and then cursed as a shot hit him in the shoulder.

Sandra had emerged from her café, sniper rifle in hand, and joined the battle.

Diego had no idea what the hell was going on, until he tackled the man all in black and, two werewolves holding him down, tore out his throat. There it was—the taste of blood that didn't quite fit, a taste he tried to avoid when possible. Vampire blood.

He transformed back and shouted to Jackson's men, "They're vampires, two of them."

"Three!" Wallace shouted, apparently having rejoined them in the square. He pointed to the far side, by Valerie, where another vampire all in black had appeared at her side with a long blade drawn.

Well this night, and all their planning, was just going to hell. The plan had been to fake her death so everyone saw, not actually kill her. If that happened, the CEOs would have won. They'd march back into the city and take it over, appointing a head of enforcement no better than Commander Strake had been.

If Diego had anything to do with it, that wasn't going to happen. He felt himself suddenly quite sobered up as he transformed again and ran to Valerie's aid.

◈ ◈ ◈

Everything was falling apart, and it didn't help that Valerie's left shoulder was burning like it was on fire. It had to have been a silver bullet—that was the only way she could figure it.

First with the shots that had made them think the plan was screwed up, and now this. She owed Sandra and the others a major apology for not letting them know when this was going down, but had felt at the time that natural reactions would be best.

Now she realized that they were probably feeling the same sense of panic she was, but worse.

At least she had kind of planned on dying that night—though a fake death would have been preferable to real.

The attacker's sword flashed and she threw herself backwards, just out of reach, and fell off of the waist-high ledge. Jackson opened up on the man, shooting with everything he had, but they had set up the rifles with regular bullets. Enough to draw blood and make the death appear real, but nothing in terms of doing real harm to a vampire if aimed correctly.

Still, Jackson knew what he was doing.

Several shots hit the attacker in the throat and he stepped back, distracted long enough for Valerie to go on the offensive.

Now was not the time to draw it out, or even to give him a second chance. Instead of going for the sword, she pushed out with her fear at the same time as she swung her arm in a wild haymaker, all her weight behind it, right for his head.

With the bullet holes already making the neck weak, her strike hit and power surging through her, she knocked the head clear off the body. She fell over with him, then glanced up to see Jackson leap onto the ledge, looking down at them.

She had to act fast, so immediately started undressing.

"Are you okay?" he hissed.

"Shoot at the ground," she replied.

"What?"

"Just do it!"

As he did, she wrapped the coat on the body, then put the pants on him. They were tight, but he was a skinny guy, and fit. She shifted to vampire speed, used the sword to hack at her hair, just the back.

"You're nuts," Jackson hissed.

"Turn around and repeat after me," she said as she dipped the hair in the guy's blood, removed his face-mask, and plastered the hair to his own. It would hold, at least for a moment or two. "She is dead, I have killed her. Oh, and grab this." She held up the sword, then added, "And this." Now she held up the head. "Get your guys up here to get rid of the body before people start asking questions."

Jackson looked like he was about to be sick, but he caught on fast.

"You know you're a little screwy in the head, right?"

"No," she held out the head, "I have no head. Go, before they wonder."

Jackson slung his rifle over his shoulder and jumped down, then took the sword and, with a cringe, the head. He turned around, stepped back up to the ledge, and held them high.

"She is dead!"

Valerie took that moment, relying on the hand-wavy fact that everyone was staring at the head that, as long as it stayed in the shadows, was hers. Pushing her vampire speed to its max, she darted around the building and out of sight, sticking to the shadows, and made her way back to the rear door of Sandra's café.

Desperately searching, she moved about the back room, then froze at a click.

She turned and breathed out—not a gun, just the door. Sandra stood there looking terrified, but the expression soon melted to relief as she ran forward and hugged Valerie. Then she hit her. And hit her again.

"You jerk!" she said. "You stupid table-licking bitch!"

"You knew about the plan!" Valerie said, holding her hands up in surrender.

"Not that it was going to be on the same night as my party."

"Yeah, that part—"

"And not the part about the damn ninjas or whatever the hell they were!"

"Actually…" Valerie shrugged. "You and me both on that one."

Sandra looked more relieved at that. "Oh, good… I shot one, and then started worrying that they were in on the plan. Well, dammit, what now?"

Valerie gestured to the fact that she wasn't wearing any pants. "This isn't very incognito, considering I'm supposed to be dead now."

"Ah, yes, your shopping bags." Sandra grabbed them

from under the washing table, and tossed Valerie a new pair of jeans and a hoody. "We're leaving tonight, I suppose?"

Valerie shook her head. "If any more of them are around, they'll be looking for us to move at night. We stay low. They were after me, not trying to cause more trouble."

"Don't worry about them," another voice said, and they jumped at the sight of Diego. "We got one more, but the one with the throat clawed out escaped. I tried to chase him, but even like that, he was too fast. I think he's leaving the city though. Realized he bit off more than he could chew."

"And Jackson?" Valerie asked.

"They're moving the body now," he said. "Threw his jacket over it, so I don't think we have anything to worry about."

"But they would've seen the other vampire attacking you, right?" Sandra asked.

"I think Jackson thought of that." Diego smiled. "I saw his people carrying away a second body in dark clothes. I imagine one of them just lay down when they got back there, and they figured he could pass until they were out of the square."

"In a way," Valerie beamed, "my plan went even better than planned. I mean, we had a *head*."

She turned to pick up the bag of clothes, and when she stood again she saw Diego cringing.

"Oh, the hair?" She shrugged. "It'll grow back. And since I won't be seeing Jackson again anytime soon anyway, who cares."

"Me for one," he said. "I'll have to see that mess every day that we're out there walking together."

"Plus, what if it doesn't?" Sandra reached out and touched it. "What if your flesh heals real fast, but your hair never does?"

She swatted Sandra's hand aside. "Shut up. Are you two ready?"

"Where are we lying low?"

"I found a place, at the outskirts of the city. Our bags, food, and everything else we need will be there, ready."

"This is really it then?" Diego shook his head, whether in disbelief or trying to clear the alcohol, Valerie couldn't be sure.

"Let's make those CEOs regret ever stepping foot in this city."

CHAPTER SEVEN

Jackson's Restaurant

The men entered behind Jackson, and the four with vampire blood either on their hands or clothes went to the bathroom or kitchen to get cleaned up.

"How the hell did they get here?" Jackson asked, spinning on them.

Baxter, the large bartender, was one of the few still there. They had figured he could serve as both muscle and screen—with his large frame in the way, it would be harder for the crowds to see who they were carrying.

He was shaking his head and said, "Could they've been local Forsaken?"

Old man Talden scoffed as he approached the bar. "Don't tell me you didn't see what they were wearing."

"Looked like ninjas."

"No, I get him," Jackson said, catching on. "It wasn't to go unrecognized, because we got a look at those faces and they aren't from around here. They wore those outfits to block out the sun."

"Does that work?" Baxter asked in amazement. "Couldn't any vampire just walk around like that then?"

"They'd look like a bunch of ninjas or lepers, but sure. Only problem is if a single bit of clothing moves, they're going to be in a world of pain. Get their clothes torn in a fight? Not so good either."

"I'm willing to bet they carried some means of shelter with them," Talden said. "As long as those UV rays don't get through, they're safe."

"It's still risky," Jackson said. "Depending on how far they came. But if they were here to kill Valerie, which I think we can all agree was their purpose, then I think we can safely assume the CEOs sent them."

"Damn, so we've got the CEOs sending assassins all the way from Chicago?" Baxter poured three glasses of whiskey, handing one to Talden and one to Jackson. He nodded to the other three men and two women. "You want something? Help yourself."

"Not necessarily Chicago." Jackson grabbed his glass and took a long sip. He set it back down and licked his lips. "Damn, that's good stuff. Point is, we don't know how far the reach of the three amigos is right now, so they could've come from anywhere, within reason."

"You don't think they're from Japan?" Baxter asked. "Like actual ninjas?"

Talden laughed at that. "Don't hurt your brain there. They weren't Japanese, first of all. Second, how would the CEOs have gotten a message out to them so fast?"

"So somewhere near Chicago then?" Baxter said, ignoring the old man's insult.

"Likely."

"I guess it doesn't really matter," Jackson said, and turned to nod at the returning men. "What we need to be focusing on now is ensuring the story sticks, and then seeing if we can get a meeting with Morgan. This city must find peace."

"If she believes you killed Valerie, she'll shake," Talden said. "I know her well enough for that. It's what she split over, after all. Just get your story straight, and we're good to go."

Jackson nodded, hoping it was true.

"That, and figure out who killed the rest of your men," a new voice said. They all turned to see Royland standing in the doorway with Cammie at his side. "Those men in the alley."

Jackson frowned. "What're you talking about?"

Cammie pushed past him and motioned to the alley behind them. Several Weres were with them, laying down the bodies that had been in the alley. Jackson felt his blood boiling, his fingers moving involuntarily.

"The gunshots we heard at the party?" he asked.

"Someone else made a move, and we don't think it could be the same vampires."

"This is one messed up night," Jackson said.

"Do we need Valerie on this?" Baxter asked.

Jackson shook his head. "She's already gone. She trusted us with this, so we're going to deal with it. But where to start." He took the drink again and finished it off, but as soon as he pulled the glass from his lips, he knew it.

"Dammit, who was in the alley? I heard some of the cops repeating who they'd found."

"Peterson," Baxter said.

"We have to check with Wallace to ensure he still has Ella locked up."

"I'm on it," Cammie said, and she went back into the alley, motioned to several of her Weres, and they were off.

◈ ◈ ◈

Enforcer HQ

Wallace lingered at the door to Ella's cell, wanting nothing more than to talk to her. She had betrayed them all, sure, but if she wanted to become a productive member of society, he wasn't going to fight that.

The question was, could she be trusted?

He threw his head back against the door in frustration, then heard the door click and felt it give.

"It's unlocked," Ella said from inside as the door opened the rest of the way.

He looked up and saw her, on the bed, leaning against the wall as if she couldn't care in the slightest that it was a prison of sorts. A prison with unlocked doors, apparently.

"You've got something on your mind?" she asked.

He opened the door and the two held eye contact. After a moment, he shook his head and said, "Did you know about this?"

"What?"

"I recognized them, Ella. I had to know, so came back without telling anyone. They were Jackson's men, and if you had anything to do with this… it's not gonna fly."

"I don't know what you're talking about."

"Ella, this is me." He stared at her from the doorway for a long while, debating how to play this, then entered and sat down on the bed beside her. Taking her hand in his, pausing only slightly at the warmth of her touch, a warmth he missed so much, he said, “If you had the chance to run away from all this, would you?”

“If I wanted to escape, I would’ve. I choose my timing.”

“I mean with me. The two of us.” He squeezed her hand, held it to his lips, breathing her in. With a kiss to the back of her hand, he said, “We could start over.”

She looked at him with a wistful smile. “My dear, I’ve already started over.”

He stared back in confusion, until her eyes moved past him and he turned to see that, behind the door, hidden in the shadows, was another man. The form stepped forward and he looked between the two. “Peterson?”

“I couldn’t leave my sister locked up,” he said. “Blood knows no bounds, isn’t that how the saying goes?”

“I’ve never heard that saying, and if so, it’s stupid.” Wallace dropped Ella’s hand, suddenly feeling less touchy-feely. “You two…?”

“We’re above this,” Peterson said. “All your bull. Shit, I heard about what happened. With Valerie dead, you all don’t stand a chance.”

Wallace, bit his lip. He wanted so bad to tell them how full of it they were, that Valerie had faked her own death and that, as much as they thought he was being had, so were they.

But instead he simply stood and walked over to his former partner.

“It’s done, Wallace,” Peterson said, pulling a pistol from his side holster.

Wallace didn’t wait for the threat. He decked him, and when he fell to the floor, Wallace turned to confront Ella—only to find a baton cracking his skull, and then it was all red and black.

CHAPTER EIGHT

Outside Old New York

As the first rays of sunlight lit the bridge leading west from Old Manhattan, Valerie stepped off of it with Sandra and Diego in tow. They all wore packs, the majority of the heavy stuff in Valerie's pack, and then Diego's. Sandra had insisted that she not be treated as less of a member of the team just because she wasn't modified, so carried a pack with mostly food and other supplies.

While the other two had checked their supplies and then repacked them, Valerie had spent the early morning hours digging into her wounds for the two silver bullets that had penetrated her flesh. At one point, Diego had to try to hold her down and help pull the bullet out, though she had sent him flying into the far wall when the pain had become unbearable.

In the end they had managed though, and Valerie had stitched herself up. As much as she hated to use some of the blood this early in the trip, she took a couple sips from one of the four vials she had brought, just to help the healing process.

Pain was her worst enemy, and right now that pain seemed to be winning. The knowledge that it would soon heal and be over with, though, helped her push on.

She had no doubts whether leaving was the right choice or not, but that didn't mean it felt good. Her friends were there, her more than friends, and a whole city she had sworn to protect. A bigger part of her thought that if she let the CEOs continue unchecked, their reach could extend far and the city would never be at peace.

The vampires who had attacked her in the night were undoubtedly sent by the CEOs, and these assassins were good. Nothing could stand against Valerie, not as far as she knew, outside of Michael, Akio, and Yuko. Still, if this Black Plague was made up of more like them? A *lot* more? That could mean trouble.

Trouble she would have to put a stop to.

"Keep us on track," Valerie said over her shoulder.

"Due west," Sandra said, holding up a creased and folded paper, the map, one of several sketched out ones that they had found in Commander Strake's old papers. It wasn't perfect, but clearly the Enforcers had mercenaries out mapping their progress as they explored and set up defensive outposts. The best they figured, the CEOs had plans for expanding at some point. Domination of America, perhaps?

Valerie slowed and glanced over her shoulder at the map. It showed a series of large lakes and, as best they could figure, Chicago was somewhere along those lakes. They had their destination, but not any great way of getting there other than their legs.

"Why couldn't we just take one of those hover car thingies?" Diego asked.

"The police pods?" Sandra asked. "Because they belong to the cops, of course."

"That, and the fact that we don't want to be seen coming," Valerie added. "If they have anyone else lingering, they might have spotted us leaving, but I doubt it. A pod heading out west is a bit more noticeable."

Diego grunted and continued walking on. They trudged in silence, and the sun rose above, soon making it annoyingly unpleasant.

A glance back showed it was much harder on Sandra. The fact that they would be eating mostly jerky and crackers, and that the walk was expected to take somewhere between a couple of weeks to a month, didn't lift Valerie's spirits much.

Still, it wasn't until around mid-afternoon that Sandra spoke up, saying she needed a break.

"What worries you most?" Diego asked.

When both women glared at him, he said, "I'm just saying… I don't worry about bears or mountain lions or whatever, I mean, we're used to that. But have either of you ever dealt with a skunk?"

"The hell's that?" Sandra asked. "Can we eat it?"

"Yeah, maybe. But if it sees you coming, you'll be stinking so bad we'll have to make you walk a mile behind us."

"Haha," she said, rolling her eyes. "You know what scares me? Mosquitoes. That and getting lost. Can you imagine just wandering around here forever until we just die from exhaustion?"

"Or boredom," Valerie chimed in, pausing to check her wounds. To her surprise and relief, they were healing nicely.

The other two turned to her, and Sandra raised an

eyebrow and said, "Boredom?"

Valerie shrugged. "When you feel like you could live forever, the idea of boredom seems a lot scarier than anything else."

They continued to stare, until finally Sandra started laughing. Soon Diego joined in.

"Did I miss something?" Valerie asked.

"Are you serious?" Sandra stood, hands in the air. "We live in a world that was destroyed by nukes or whatever the hell happened, where vampires and Weres roam the earth, where men and women kill like it's fun, and for some of them it is, and here you are worried about boredom?"

"It's too good," Diego added, wiping a laughing-tear from his eye.

"Yeah, well… it's better than skunks and mosquitos."

Diego smirked and said, "Well, it used to be that I'd drink the wrong water and shit myself to death."

They laughed and Sandra said, "Gross."

"True story," he said. "I saw it happen to a guy but then… I realized that I was a Were, and my stomach could heal from whatever I gave it. So, not a worry anymore."

Valerie and Diego both suddenly stopped smiling, and turned to Sandra.

"What?" Sandra asked. "Oh, because I'm not a vampire or Were. Yeah, don't worry, I don't plan on death by shitting – which is completely gross by the way, so… yeah. I'll keep my worry to mosquitos, you two protect me from everything else."

"You don't, I don't know, want to see if…?" Diego looked to Valerie for help here, but she just frowned and shook her head. She'd brought up the topic of changing Sandra before, and knew Sandra wasn't open to it.

In truth, it worried Valerie too. The chances of surviving the transformation to vampire for anyone were low, especially so for females, for some reason. They didn't die, but lost their minds. The results were the mindless creatures they called Nosferatu. She wasn't sure if it was the same for Weres, but didn't really want her friend to take the risk.

"This is who I am," Sandra said, and stood, cinching on her pack. Without another word, she started walking.

"Sensitive topic?" Diego asked Valerie.

She nodded, put on her own pack, and followed.

CHAPTER NINE

Enforcer HQ

The night hadn't been especially kind to any of them, but at least Royland was used to being up at night and sleeping during the day. After forming teams and spreading out through the city, they had failed to find any more of the assassins, and the one that ran seemed to have escaped.

While there were walls around the city, they only really helped against the whackos and nomad tribes, neither of which had bothered Old Manhattan in some time. A skilled assassin, especially of the vampire variety, wouldn't find it incredibly difficult to find a section of the wall that was unguarded and climb up.

Unguarded was the key there—now Cammie had her team of Weres out searching along the wall to ensure no guards had been casualties in the night.

All of that aside, the fake death of Valerie had worked.

Already word was spreading that the would-be liberator turned attacker was done for at the hands of Jackson, and that the city leaders were rallying behind him.

That only left Morgan and her underground fighters.

Which was why Royland was walking along the hallway to Ella's room in the early hours of the morning. He meant to arrange a meeting with them on his terms. The way he figured it, Morgan couldn't fight the whole city, and Ella was their only means of communication with her.

Only, when he reached the room, the door was wide open.

A pair of legs were just visible in the corner.

Royland burst into the room, ready for trouble, but instead only found Wallace. The man wore his police uniform and had a lump on the back of his head. He must have been hit hard.

"Wallace, you with me?"

A groan came in response.

Royland hefted the man up, which wasn't especially hard given Royland's vampire strength, despite his exhaustion. He sped out of there and to the elevators, where at this point, Wallace was recovering but had a dazed look. While they waited, the man even looked like he was about to vomit.

"Dammit, Wallace, what happened?" Royland asked. "You might be concussed. Ella did this to you?"

Wallace nodded and muttered a, "Uh-huh."

"I don't get it, she was just starting to earn our trust."

The doors opened and there were two of his vampires. They took a moment to process the scene, and one said, "Medical?"

"Please." He guided Wallace in, so that the other two could support him, and said, "I'm going to wake the colonel."

"No need," the other vampire said. "Saw a figure on the roof on our way in, and I'm pretty sure it was him."

Royland nodded his thanks and made for the stairs, bounding up them two at a time. With each step he cursed their luck. First the assassin situation, though that could have gone way worse, and now this with Ella escaping. When he made it all the way to the top, he was winded and pissed, so the door went flying open with a bang, though he didn't mean it to.

Colonel Donnoly spun on him, hand on the pistol at his side. "Damn, Royland. Should we just pile a heart attack onto everything else?"

"Ella's gone, sent Wallace to medical."

"The hell?" Donnoly released the pistol, both hands on the railing as he leaned back to look out over the city. "That's why love doesn't belong in the workplace."

"Or why we shouldn't give any leeway to those who have betrayed us in the past."

"You don't believe in second chances, Royland?"

"Sir, I'm a vampire, a former Forsaken taken in by the kindness of Valerie after she rescued me. If anyone here believes in second chances, it's me. That doesn't mean we just hand them out like butterscotch at a birthday party."

"Butterscotch at a..." Donnoly turned to stare at him, frowning. "Exactly how long have you been around?"

Royland shrugged. "Long enough."

Donnoly shrugged, apparently accepting it, and returned to assessing the city. Even with his head spinning with all that was happening, Royland had to admit that the city looked peaceful. The sun hadn't risen yet, though the dark blue on the horizon was turning yellow, and a low fog was settling over the taller buildings, theirs included. Wisps of it passed as they watched.

"I hope you have a plan," Royland finally said.

"Letting the Weres and vampires deal with it isn't enough, I suppose."

Royland chuckled. "You want to deal with something in the UnknownWorld, you come to us. Something's going on with you Regulars, seems to me that's your territory."

"Regulars?"

"Not to be confused with Regulators, yes. I figure that's what you all are, right? We're genetically modified humans, you're not. You're regular. Borings could work too, but I went with the more PC version."

"I'll be sure to thank you for that someday," Donnoly said. He turned to Royland and took a deep breath, eyes roaming across the vampire's face. "I trust you, which is saying a lot. It wasn't that long ago I didn't know vampires really existed, you know? I heard legends, rumors from the pirates we'd arrested over the years. They say there's a vampire king up there, you know that? That he lives in the deep north, and that pirates give him treasure and the occasional sacrifice, or he will swarm down on them with his vampire horde."

"Well, shit…" was all Royland could think to say.

"Shit indeed. I never believed it until I met you. All those symbols on the pirate ships, of vampire skulls and worse, I always assumed it was simply part of their image. Intimidation factors. Now I'm starting to wonder just how screwed up the north really is." He turned to Royland and frowned. "Something funny?"

"I hadn't even realized I was smiling," Royland said. "But no, I was just thinking how we here in America tried to stay so secret, while all this time we could've been up north terrorizing pirates."

"Maybe you'll get your chance someday."

"No, my place is here with you and the people of Old Manhattan."

"And that's why I like you." Donnoly clapped him on the shoulder. "But here's the thing. A messenger arrived just half an hour ago, from Morgan. She wants to set up a meeting with us and Jackson. I guess she heard about Valerie's so-called Death."

"That and her most recent power play with Ella, if the two were connected."

"Oh, I'm sure they are."

The two turned to head back down, Royland's mind spinning with what this meeting could be about.

CHAPTER TEN

Fallen Lands Outpost

Robin and Brad were on their first raid and it was exhilarating. The mission, as Giuseppe had laid it out, was to gather supplies, additional weapons and ammo from one of the nearby City States. It was much less protected, scouts reported, and if anything it seemed to be hostile toward the FDG.

That's how she could justify it—they were hurting the FDG's enemy, so that they would have a better chance when it comes to taking us on. Even the odds before slaughtering them.

The idea of killing anyone still sat sour in Robin's mouth. She had been training night after night, learning all of the weapons at their disposal, and occasionally beating the piss out of Brad—not that he didn't get his in as well—but killing was different.

Sinking one's vampire teeth into a person's neck and

feeding, as they told her she would have to do, went against everything she believed in. Once she went there, could she ever go back? Could she really return to her family someday and look them in the eyes, after committing such an atrocity?

Not likely.

They moved under the pale moon, careful not to be seen until it was time. They chose this location, thirty miles or so outside of Chicago, because it was close enough for word and terror to spread, but far enough away to make the FDG question the stories they would hear.

This far away also meant the CEOs could keep their hands clean. They were relatively new to the area, and attacks soon after their arrival could earn finger pointing their way. Not that they didn't have the armies to stand their ground.

It was a different sort of city than Robin was used to seeing, out here in the trees with wooden stakes protruding from the ground and huge crosses, as if either would really deter their kind.

There had been a time when she too wondered if the old religions would do anything to fend off vampires. She had learned the hard way that nothing could keep the vampires away once they were determined to kill or take a city.

Now she was on the other side, Brad nearby, a handful of other newer vampires trailing behind.

A shout sounded in the night, and she spun to see the shadow of a man falling from the wall, one of Brad's vampires already making his move.

"Control your team," she said, but realized it was too late for that now. She motioned her team forward, and they sprinted, full on vampire speed, to take the walls and anyone who stood in their way.

Robin, for her part, was up and over the wall before

anyone had time to process what had happened, and found herself in a make-shift city built largely on old ruins, but with a few log cabins and even several tents and teepees.

It actually would have been a pleasant place to live, before becoming a vampire.

"FEED!" a loud voice called, and she turned to see Giuseppe on the wall now, three of his vampires behind him, watching as if this were a great show.

But it wasn't part of the plan. They were supposed to enter, take supplies, and return, only killing if necessary.

And then, as a man emerged from a nearby tent, ax in hand, she realized that this was still training. The element of surprise. The need to kill, as they would be too exhausted from the trip and the fighting to otherwise stand a chance.

She hated them at that moment, even as she dodged a strike from the man with the ax, and then plowed into him with her shoulder. He flew back into the tent, collapsing it and hitting something metal that was inside. As he recovered, two more emerged from houses nearby, one with a crossbow and one with two knives.

This wasn't going to end well for anyone. Either she'd be killed, or have to kill, and it pissed her off.

With a hiss, she charged them and swept out the legs of the knife-holder, then felt a crossbow bolt take her in the calf. She grunted in pain and turned on the guy, leaping forward to backhand him and send him spiraling into the dirt.

More men and several women were appearing to join the fight, but soon vampires were plowing through them, pausing momentarily to bite into them and replenish their energy through feeding.

Blood splattered the ground, and Robin found herself both sickened to her stomach and filled with an odd yearning.

She pushed it aside, spinning as she witnessed the carnage. Her calf stung horribly, and when the man came at her with a sword she barely reacted in time to dodge the blow.

The next strike came heavy and from the right, so that when she stepped to dodge out of the way, forgetting she was injured, her leg gave out. The sword swung inches from her head, and she scampered backward and away from the attacking man.

If anyone saw her retreating, she would be toast. Right now though, that didn't matter. Her chest rose and fell in quick bursts and she felt a cold sweat on the sides of her neck, just below the ears.

The next sword strike came but hit the wood of a doorway. Using the moment to escape, Robin rolled back and planted herself in a defensive stance, hissing with red eyes glowing to scare the man off.

He hesitated, and in that second a vampire from outside slit his throat and then fell on the man, consuming his life.

No matter what Robin did here, she realized, it didn't matter. These people were goners.

But it would not be by her hand.

A whimper came from behind. Slowly turning her head, she came face to face with a woman about her own age with wide, teary eyes.

"It's okay," Robin said. "I'm not going to…"

Something had slid into her midsection, cold and sharp, and when she looked down she saw the woman clutching a cooking knife half plunged into Robin's torso. With another whimper, the woman shifted the blade, turning it in an attempt to ensure it did its worst.

Unbelievable pain shot through Robin and rage filled her, but she fought it.

"Go, get out of here," she whispered, taking the woman's hands and pulling the knife out, "while you still can."

The woman's hands trembled, but she tried to stab Robin again.

This time Robin reacted, slapping the knife out of the woman's hands, before stumbling back and plopping onto her butt. She stared up at the woman as her own blood flowed, and once again said, "Go!"

A shadow fell through the doorway, and the woman turned with terror-filled eyes.

In a flash, she was on the floor, Brad holding her by the neck, snarling.

He looked between her and Robin with confusion, then his eyes widened with realization.

"They'll kill you," he said to her, eyes pleading. "They'll drain you and leave you for dead, or worse, if you don't take her life." He leaned back, hand still on the woman's throat, and said, "You have to drink."

The woman's eyes went wide and she tried to scream, but Brad's hand moved to her mouth. It wouldn't have mattered anyway, with the screams and sounds of fighting outside.

Still, for Robin it mattered. This was a person, not some animal for the slaughter.

"I won't," she whispered. With a spasm of pain, she tried to back away, but the pool of blood beneath her was spreading and she slipped.

The pain and exhaustion were worse than she thought, and as she tried to stand again, she collapsed, head hitting the floor, hard.

"You've never fed before," Brad said, frustration burning in his voice. "Of course… and with all we've been doing, you're drained. Robin, please."

She shook her head.

He grunted in frustration, then pulled the helpless woman up beside him, hand still over her mouth.

"You want to be with your family again someday, right?" He glared at her, chest heaving. "Yes, I know much more about you than you'd think. And I know that you don't want to let this end here. That you can't stand the idea of your mother and father out there, never knowing what happened to you. Nor you passing on without having another chance to hug them, tell them you love them, am I right?"

Clenching her teeth, she nodded. Dammit, he was right. But not like this.

"DO IT!" he shouted, thrusting the woman forward, who collapsed on her knees in tears.

Robin shook her head, barely, though it took an effort.

"Ah!" Brad stepped forward, took the woman's wrist, and bit in, deep. For a moment he drank, dark red blood trickling down his chin as he closed his eyes in ecstasy, and then, when the woman was too weak to resist, he held the wrist to Robin's mouth and pressed.

When she tried to push it away, he pressed harder, and then the first drop of blood hit her tongue and she didn't realize it, but she was clinging to the arm, drinking and feeling each heartbeat of this woman, growing slower, and slower.

At last she pushed back, screaming as her back arched and she screamed in frustration at what she had become. At what Brad had made her become.

"Not me," Brad said, pulling her close and pointing to the doorway. "Them, Robin. Never forget it was them who did this to us."

Robin glared, on the verge of exploding, but then glanced at the near lifeless form of the woman on the floor.

"She's not dead," Brad whispered. "By morning, she might be, or maybe not. The point is that you live to fight another day… to find your family."

All Robin could do was stare at the woman's body, her chest barely rising and falling at all, her fingers twitching.

Finally, unable to watch any longer, Robin pushed herself up and turned to the door, where she froze at the sight of Giuseppe standing there. His eyes were glowing red, his fangs exposed, and he smiled.

"Well done, children," he said, and then motioned for them to follow as he spun and disappeared into the now silent darkness.

"Robin," Brad said, reaching out a hand to comfort her, "you know it had to be done."

She stepped out of his reach and glared. "Whether it did or not, that won't change the disgust I feel right now when I look at you."

"Then let's hope time truly heals all wounds," he said. "Because I never plan on leaving your side."

With a shiver, full of revulsion, she turned and walked out of there with Brad in tow.

In the midst of ruins and log cabins and teepees, the vampires were gathered, along with a batch of fresh supplies. Many had blood on their chins or splattered across their clothes, all but one. A man Robin recognized from only having arrived about a week after her. He stood defiantly, looking at the rest of them with disgust.

"This, my warriors, my beautiful assassins of the night," Giuseppe said, "is what happens when you fail to embrace your calling."

In a swift, unnatural motion, Giuseppe was behind the vampire, hand on his throat, and then he tore it out. The vampire fell to his knees, gasping for air as he bled out, but Giuseppe wasn't done. He drew his weapon, a large cudgel of a sword, and then brought it down hard on the back of the vampire's neck, so that the head went rolling.

Robin covered her mouth at the taste of bile, and she felt the trees around them spinning.

In spite of her hatred and disgust for Brad at that moment, another feeling crept in—gratitude. As much as she despised what he had done for her, the others had assumed she had fed on her own, so she was still alive.

As he had said, he saved her life.

She would be sure to repay him by surviving long enough to really escape and find her family again.

CHAPTER ELEVEN

Fallen Lands

Valerie's bullet wounds were healing well, which was a relief considering that she had to be conservative with the vials of blood.

That didn't make the trudge any more bearable. God, she thought she hated pain? Well, that was only because she had never been able to compare it to true boredom. This never-ending journey across the land that was at times arid, at others swampy. The world after the collapse of society was nothing if not confusing.

And to make it worse, Sandra and Diego were being their normal, sappy selves. What had she been thinking, letting them come with her?

More than once, as she walked on ahead to scout the area and ensure there weren't any nomad groups or worse, she considered just telling them to turn back while she ran off in the other direction, too fast for them to catch up.

But she didn't have it in her. What if they never made it back? She'd be on her return trip, successful, only to find their skeletons by the side of the road. It wasn't a chance she was willing to take.

So, she walked… and walked… and walked.

Her ears perked up. What was that? For the first time—silence.

She turned back to see Sandra and Diego walking, but neither talking. Her smile didn't go unnoticed, before she quickly turned back and kept on.

"What was that?" Sandra asked.

"Just enjoying all this nature," Valerie called back.

It wasn't a complete lie. Their surroundings, for the first time in over an hour, were quite pleasant. Instead of the fields of dead grass they'd traversed for the last thirty minutes, now they had reached a valley that had accumulated enough water for a small river. Lush trees rose up on each side, and even continued on past the valley a ways.

As they made their way through trees and around clumps of blackberry bushes, tall ferns, and the occasional fallen tree, they heard a low humming.

Valerie held up a hand then motioned forward. She walked slowly, careful not to step on twigs.

The humming grew louder, stopped, then started up again. A glance back showed, Sandra and Diego, eyes narrowed with interest. Funny how Sandra's eyes would have once conveyed fear. After all they had been through their safety apparently wasn't as much of a concern as it used to be.

Out here where they didn't know what could be waiting, that might not be the safest attitude.

They came to a drop-off where a large outcropping of rocks held up the earth, and several trees had grown, which provided cover for them to watch. Below, wading through the river, were men and women in what looked like burlap sacks. They hummed and chanted, and several in the middle carried a man, nude but for a cloth placed over his lower half.

"Dead," Sandra whispered, and Valerie nodded in confirmation.

With a final chant, the group lowered the wooden carrier with the body into the water, then stood vigilant as it floated off.

Soon the burlap-sack wearing people began to wander off, each in their own time. When the last had gone, Valerie leaned against the large rock. She took out some jerky and handed it around.

"We can push on," Sandra said. "They don't seem like the type we have to worry about."

"It's not that." Valerie turned and looked in the direction the body had gone. The water sparkled gold in spots where the sunlight trickled down between leaves. "So many bodies in Old Manhattan just tossed into dumpsters. It feels a bit wrong."

"Some have gone into the ocean," Diego said with a shrug. "Oh, and Mecha, we gave him a proper burial."

"Yes, I guess you did."

"Something on your mind?" Sandra asked, pausing to chew so that she could assess her friend.

"I'm just ready for the violence to end, is all. Of course I'm happy to see justice done, but when can I stop? When can I sit back and say that everything's as it should be, and they have no more need of me?"

"That's what you want?" Diego asked. "To not be needed?"

"If it means more people living in peace, then yes."

He looked away, and shrugged. “It won’t ever really end, Valerie. There will always be evil people popping up.”

She shook her head. “You don’t understand. It might never end completely, but part of why I left Cammie and the others in control was that I believe they can do what must be done.”

“And then where would you go?” Sandra asked.

“We,” Valerie corrected her.

But Sandra glanced at Diego, then back to Valerie, and bit her lip.

“Ah, the three of us then,” Valerie added. “I never know.”

“We can talk about it more at the time,” Sandra said, earning her a glare from Diego.

Valerie hadn’t considered that there would be something more to discuss. The hesitant look in Sandra’s eyes told it all—her home was in Old Manhattan now. It was where she had come to care for Diego, and it was where she became her own woman.

Maybe Valerie didn’t need to leave either, but… she was *dead* there, after all. At least, she had hopefully convinced the majority of the population that she was. If it helped bring out Morgan and any resistance fueled by hatred for her, or at least threw the CEOs off her scent, it would be worth it. But returning to live a normal life? Not exactly the easiest thing to do at this point.

She sure hoped that little experiment paid off.

“Come on,” Valerie said, standing and pulling her pack around to grab a couple of the now empty canteens.

“You want to get water from there?” Sandra asked.

“Of course.”

“But it had a dead person in it!”

Valerie laughed. “Dear, the water moves. We can go

upstream. The point is, we have no idea when the next clean water source will come along. This could be the last water source you'll see for days."

Sandra looked horrified, but they went to the water, refilled the canteens, and then were soon on their way again.

On the other side of the valley, the trees were sparser, but the air was pleasant. The rays of sunshine tickled Valerie's skin and she was reminded how she had only recently become able to walk about in the day.

Then a thought hit her—Michael had given her these powers, told her he might come back for her. She frowned, wondering what would happen if he returned while she was out dealing with the CEOs, or some other matter.

Would he wait? Would he have some way of tracking her down? Or… did it even matter?

Part of her felt that he had always intended this for her, and he was still trying to figure out his plan for the world as he went. Yes, he would take out The Duke, her creator, in France. But then what? Yuko and Akio would eventually find him, and then they would rejoin Bethany Anne, she supposed.

That sounded great and all, but she wasn't sure where she fit into the picture. Up in outer space, serving as some sort of soldier in the war against alien forces? Or maybe she would stay here as Michael's sentry on earth.

Either way, a normal life and settling down and all that didn't seem to be in her stars. For Diego and Sandra, however, it was. She knew that.

And this knowledge made her sad at the realization that the three of them wouldn't always be together. That life, or fate, or whatever dictated so much of where you went and, in fact, it could all be over at any moment.

With a glance back, she slowed and offered a smile.

"What's up with the silly grin?" Diego asked.

"Just… it's not the worst thing in the world that you two came along."

Sandra laughed and nudged Diego. "That's her way of saying, 'You two are the most amazing people in the world, I'm so lucky to be here with you.'"

"Aw, that's sweet," Diego said with a chuckle.

"Shut up," Valerie waved them off, but her smile didn't falter. She looked over at the rock face lining the surrounding hills, hoping they wouldn't have to climb it. "You two are like family, you know? The closest thing I have to it, anyway."

The other two nodded, and Diego said, "We're all the closest thing we have to family."

"Screw that," Sandra said. "We are family. There's no getting around it."

They kept walking and, when night settled, they found a small cave in the rock face. Diego got a low fire going just outside the cave for Sandra, then sat with an arm around her.

"It's been a long time since I had family," he said, staring into the flames.

"At least you didn't kill yours," Valerie said, thinking back to Donovan. "Wait, did you?"

He shook his head with a chuckle, "No, I'm glad to say I didn't. But… neither did you, really. Right?"

She scrunched her nose, thinking. "Huh, I guess you're right. He wasn't my real brother, just my vampire brother. Created by the same vampire. It's been so long now, it's all become a kind of blur."

"If I had a brother, I think he'd be something like that new Were," Sandra said. "The one who rescued you, Diego. What was his name?"

"Ricky? How so?"

"You know, big so he can protect me. Gay, so he doesn't try to hit on my girlfriends."

"Considering I'm your only girlfriend," Valerie said, "and that I'm kind of single at the moment, in a way, would that be so bad?"

Sandra shrugged. "I just don't want you hooking up with my brother, that's all."

"Wait a minute." Diego pulled back from her, his brow furrowed. "I'm not big, and I can protect you."

"First of all, you're big where it counts, honey—"

"Ew!" Valerie waved. "Guys, I'm right here, okay?"

"As if you haven't seen it all." Sandra smirked and squeezed Diego's leg playfully, causing him to blush. "And second, my big, strong defender… I don't need you to protect me. That was just a brother thing, you know. I mean like, growing up it would've been nice to have a big, strong brother. Now I have Junior here." She patted her sniper rifle and smiled.

"But I would protect you, if you ever needed it," Diego said, apparently unable to let it go.

"And I, you," she said, and gave Valerie a look that she interpreted to mean what they all knew—if it really came down to it, they all knew Valerie would be doing the majority of the protecting.

They rested there in the cave, with Valerie taking the majority of the watch. Diego relieved her in the early morning though, and she had to admit she needed rest. As soon as she leaned up against the cave wall, Sandra curled up beside her, she was asleep.

A clattering woke her and she sprang for her sword, but Diego was there with a wide-eyed look and said, "It's just me! Apparently, this area has rabbits."

"You saw one?" she asked.

"Better." He held up two already skinned and cooked hares. "I did a bit of hunting."

She had always been partial to the little guys, so didn't feel too great about eating. But then again, she knew jerky was going to get old fast. Sandra, however, dug in as if she hadn't eaten in days, not even bothering to wipe the grease from her chin until she was done.

"Never thought you'd get to see this side of each other, huh?" Valerie asked Diego with a wink.

"This side?" He looked from Valerie to Sandra, then smiled, catching on. "Oh, the grease and all that?"

"Not showering, eating like an animal… yeah."

"You forget, I'm a Were. All that kinda turns me on."

"Gross." Valerie turned, pulling together their supplies so they could get back on the road. "Really, just… disgusting. Both of you."

Sandra glanced at Valerie's unfinished meal. "Does that mean you won't be having yours?"

"Go for it."

"And maybe you can give us twenty minutes?" Diego said. When she looked at him with confusion, he winked and added, "Alone?"

"What? No, fuck no. You two wanted to come on this trip, I mean join me on this journey, so no, no coming on this trip."

"Talk about vulgar assumptions," Sandra said, scoffing. She turned to Diego with a raised eyebrow. "Unless…?"

He smiled and nodded. "Yeah, that's exactly what I was inferring. She was dead on."

Sandra laughed and stood, finally finished. "Okay, you might get turned on by all this wild living, but this girl needs a bath and some rose water to spray on myself before we can even think about five minutes, let alone twenty." She sniffed. "Honestly, you stink, and so do I."

"It doesn't bother me, so—"

"Nuh-uh, it bothers me. And it bothers Valerie that we're even talking about this. Look at the flush in her cheeks."

"Bullshit, I'm not blushing." Valerie turned and walked out of there, rolling her eyes. Yeah, she had totally been blushing. But also getting kinda pissed. She'd given up her right to get some when she set off on this mission, so it wasn't fair for them to be so open in front of her.

The following days went by without anything out of the ordinary happening. Sandra started to complain about blisters, but whenever Diego or Valerie got them, they would heal, so it was hard to commiserate.

One morning it started to rain, and didn't give up for three whole days. Since they hadn't thought about bringing any sort of raincoats, Valerie scouted ahead and spotted an abandoned barn.

They hunkered down in there, put on dry clothes, and waited it out.

"What if the rain goes on for months?" Sandra asked on the third day.

"I don't think so," Valerie said, standing next to her. She sniffed the air, and Diego did the same. "You too?"

He nodded. "It's like, out here and away from all the city smells, you can almost smell the weather changes.

Sure enough, within an hour the sun was out, and they found themselves chasing a rainbow. None of them talked of gold at the end of it though, Valerie noted. That was a fun belief left over from the old days, still strong as ever, but they all knew the treasure that awaited them, and that treasure was called justice. She meant to bring judgment to the CEOs, and see that they paid for their pasts.

A light mist swirled in around midday, and then the sun won out again and the result was a muggy humidity. They pushed on through it, only stopping to rest for a snack, until the evening. Soon the sun was beginning its descent and casting streaks of bright pink and purple through the clouds above.

Valerie was just starting to think they should veer off the route Sandra had them on and find somewhere to rest, when they spotted what was no doubt once a big city in the foreground, a large lake beyond.

"Huh," Sandra said, turning the map in her hand and glancing around. "I'm not really sure. It doesn't feel like we've been walking long enough to have reached Chicago, does it?"

Diego shook his head, and Valerie had to agree.

"I doubt it," she said. "Even at our rate."

"That would make this any random city along the way," Sandra said, "or possibly Cleveland, Ohio."

"Only one way to find out," Valerie said. "Ask."

She started off toward the city, determined to march in there and find out where they were and how much farther they had to go.

CHAPTER TWELVE

Old Manhattan

The neutral location chosen by Morgan was at an old warehouse by the docks, close to where Jackson imagined Valerie would have arrived when she first came to America. Damn, he missed her. But it wasn't time to dwell on emotions, and seldom was in this world.

No, it was time to take care of business.

He checked over his shoulder and received nods from Baxter and Talden. Lorain had stayed back at the restaurant for this, but he had others nearby ready for when the moment came.

He paused at the entryway to the warehouse, very aware that they could've just set this up to bomb him and everyone else that showed. It certainly wasn't the first time Morgan's people had made the attempt.

Not a single sign of foul play though, so he motioned to the others and entered.

There she was, Morgan, with her strikingly red hair up in a bun, wearing her telltale green dress and with a distinctly out of place shotgun at her side.

"For insurance," she said, patting the weapon fondly.

He looked around, seeing that Morgan had brought many faces he knew, those who had betrayed him. Now they looked at him curiously. They all wondered if he was going to really be okay with this, he imagined. They knew him too well.

"You actually did it," Morgan said with a slight smile. "Seems the old Jackson is back."

"The old Jackson?" he asked.

"Ruthless. Unafraid to take a life when it was for the greater good." She motioned to those around her. "And now, we're yours again. I think we can all agree this is for the greater good."

It was all he could do not to lose it right then and there. How dare she talk about Valerie's death like that? Even if she hadn't really died, this woman didn't know that. A second thought hit him as he glanced around.

"Ella and Peterson, where are they?"

Morgan's eyes showed confusion for a moment, then her mask of a smile returned. "Yes, they're waiting for this to be over before returning."

Jackson was pretty sure that look in her eyes had meant she had no idea, which meant Peterson and Ella hadn't gone straight to them. But if not Morgan and her crew, the only underground remaining, then where?

"So how will this work?" Morgan asked. "Your people have been notified? The Weres and vampires will leave?"

"Don't worry, they know exactly what they're supposed to do," Jackson said. He glanced over to a dark movement in the corner and then behind him. "I'll just give them the final order, and when it's over they won't concern you ever again."

He ignored her annoying smile as he turned and walked for the door. With each step, he waited for her betrayal, but it didn't come. Considering what he had planned, he almost wished she had tried to shoot him in the back.

At the doorway, he nodded to Cammie, who waited just outside. She winked in an almost flirtatious way, tipped the cowboy hat she had put on for this special occasion, and moved in.

"What the fu—" a voice called from inside, but he was walking away, leaving the Weres to their revenge.

He paused, listening to gunshots, yelps, snarls, and thudding of bodies against walls.

She had been right, he thought. The old Jackson was back.

Before he had met Valerie, he had been much stricter on revenge and seeing that peace won out, no matter what the cost. As she had said, "Ruthless. Unafraid to take a life when it was for the greater good."

But it was the opposite of what she thought. She was the darkness that needed to be cast from this world so that the greater good could shine.

And Cammie and her Weres had met the hot side of Morgan's explosives one too many times to allow any sort of truce. The trust simply wasn't there, and never would be.

Would Valerie have approved? He didn't think so. But what was done was done.

◈ ◈ ◈

Royland stood at the edge of the waterway, alone, staring out over the red and yellow reflections of flames that had risen up over the warehouse. It was done, as Cammie had told him it would be.

He hated the thought of revenge, when the other side had set aside their weapons. Or, maybe hadn't exactly set them aside, but was holding out a hand for peace.

It reminded him too much of his days as a Forsaken. It was too close to the moral boundary for him, and so he needed time to think.

The fire brigade would arrive soon, but there was nothing they would be able to do at this point.

With a pain in the back of his skull, he turned and walked away from the water and into the city. At first, he thought he would go to Sandra's café. He loved it there, after all. But he didn't want to be seen by anyone who knew him, as that meant talking.

Instead he took a turn north, wandering to see where he would end up. Soon he found himself at the edge of the old hotels, the ones where many of the homeless or drugged out found themselves staying.

He thought he remembered Valerie mentioning a crazy fight that had broken out here with them involved, before they had rescued him from having his blood drained. Those were insane times. He was glad to be moving on, but scared that Valerie's absence would pull this city back into the muck she'd found it in.

"Is it so bad?" a voice asked. He started before turning to see Cammie. She stood in the shadows of a nearby building, biting her lip as she looked out at him.

"You following me?"

She nodded. "You were right."

He just frowned, refusing to give her the satisfaction of him asking what about.

With a sideway glance, she added, "About all that back there. Does it feel good to know those ass-faces are dead, so they can't backstab anyone again or catch us in random explosions? Most definitely. But the whole revenge angle? Not so much."

"We're different, Cammie."

"Maybe… maybe not."

He frowned and turned back to the hotels, watching as two men started arguing in the distance. One punched the other, knocking him to the ground before turning to storm off into the hotel.

"This is how the city lives," Royland said. "We have to work together to see them through these dark times."

"Royland." She stepped forward, reaching for his arm, but he pulled away. After a moment of staring at him, she clucked her tongue. "That's how it is then?"

"Like I said, we're different."

"Maybe not so different."

He took the bait this time, and asked, "How do you figure?"

"Yeah, I let my Weres do their business, I even had Morgan in my grasp for a second… but couldn't do it. You're right, I mean, killing since Valerie changed up the town, it's become a necessity from time to time, but this, it just felt wrong."

"So she's alive?"

"God, no. I let her go and she tried to pull that shotgun on me, so Ricky tore her to shreds. I'm not saying I didn't feel the thrill of it all, but what I can say is that I'm with you now."

He scoffed. "Does it matter? What enemies do we have left?"

"Every criminal still on the streets is our enemy," she said.

"Until they abandon their old ways, and then become one of us, that is. And then, of course, there's the pirates."

"Those bastards, I might not have a problem tearing them to shreds."

She laughed. "Keep talking dirty, I like it."

"If that turns you on, well… first, that's a little disturbing. Second, I wonder how turned on you'll get when you actually see what I do to them."

"No mercy there? For real?"

He shook his head. "Well, mercy if they ask for it. Pirates don't strike me as the type to do so."

They both turned to the sky, east across the ocean where they could see one of the ships moving out of port and circling to head west.

"Ella, oh my God," Cammie said. She grabbed Royland's arm and this time he didn't pull away. "They might be escaping via the blimps."

"Back up a step. Ella wasn't with Morgan and the resistance?"

She shook her head. "I think her and Peterson have something else planned, and now that we're talking about it, that only makes sense. If she wanted to fight, she would have stayed and joined Morgan again. Fleeing on foot would be troublesome, but if they escaped via blimp, that would be a whole other story.

"But she was helping with the raids," Royland said. "I don't understand—"

"Sure, to keep the fighting going. To keep us all distracted."

Royland nodded, catching on. "And now she's become a mercenary for all we know, her and her brother selling their swords to the highest bidder?"

"That part doesn't sound like her, but… come on, if she

did go to the docks, we might still be able to catch her."

They started to run, but Royland pulled her back by the hand. She glanced down at their hands touching raised an eyebrow and tilted her hat.

"Is now really the time for that?" she said with a chuckle.

He rolled his eyes. "No, it's just, what then? If we catch her?"

Cammie frowned, then shook her head. "I don't know. But I promise, no harm, not unless we find out she means to harm the city."

"Deal," he said, shaking her hand and then dropping it.

She glanced back at her empty hand, then put on a fake pout. "Talk about your major let downs."

"Just try to keep up," he said, and took off in a run toward the docks.

"You're the one who seems to have trouble keeping up," Cammie said, running alongside him. "All these hints that I'm into you, heck, even changing my ways for you, kinda, and you're too dense to follow."

"Changing because of me," he said, "not for me. And I'm following, it's just that I'm waiting for a moment to make the first move, see. And since you're always trying, it hasn't given me an opening."

She laughed. "Tell you what, after this is done I'll just lay back and keep my mouth shut, and see if you can find an opening."

He did a double take, but even she was blushing. "You didn't mean it that way, did you?"

"No, but… it's pretty funny."

They both cracked up laughing as they ran. Royland couldn't believe that she was able to make him feel this way in the midst of everything else going on, but damn, it felt good.

CHAPTER THIRTEEN

Black Plague HQ

Robin had hoped they would be done with the testing and training that night when Brad had forced her to feed, but she soon learned they would never truly be finished.

She was at a higher level now, training right alongside Giuseppe and others she had seen around. It turned out he was the leader of her group of recruits, but there were at least a dozen like him. Each had been charged with forming a group of warrior vampires, training them for assaults on cities or assassinations, so they would be ready to address whatever needs arose.

He had been relatively successful with his group of vampire recruits. Most others only had half his numbers, while one had only been able to make Nosferatu. This one had been taken out of the main group, and ordered to work on manipulating the Nosferatu to the point that they would be ready for battle.

They worked hard, but even worse, they partied hard.

Nights were filled with drinking—not that it had much of an effect on vampires, but that's why they enjoyed the good stuff. A local stash of old, basement made moonshine was their choice of drink. A vampire would chug it, act like an idiot for a few minutes, and then sober up as their healing process worked the alcohol out of their systems.

No hangovers either, Robin supposed.

This night she found herself at the outskirts of the most recent outpost that they had destroyed, watching as flames licked the sky and vampires danced through the red, glowing streets. The night air was filled with the scent of smoke and blood, and the crackling of burning houses was almost peaceful in a horrifying way.

"Here you are," Brad said, stumbling over, a bottle of the light green drink in his hand. "What, not in the mood?"

"Never."

He looked at her, frowning with an unfocused stare, then sobered up. He took another swig.

"What do you want?" she asked. "Go on, enjoy your party."

A man shrieked nearby, followed by a vampire's laughter. It sent a shudder through Robin.

"We've done it, haven't we?" he asked.

"Done what?"

"Survived."

She frowned, looking from him to the flames and revelry. A vampire held a man on his lap, two puncture marks on the man's throat.

"You call this survival?" She shook her head. "It's disgusting."

He stared at her, eyes narrowed and lips moving as if

he were thinking up a response and trying to say it, but the words weren't coming.

Finally, he stepped forward, grabbed her by the waist, and pulled her in for a kiss. The smell of liquor was strong on his breath.

"Agh!" She exclaimed, stepping back and pushing him away. "What the hell?"

He frowned, and then did it again. This time, she side-stepped and left a leg in his path, so that he went toppling over. Moonshine splattered the dirt as the bottle shattered, and when Brad stood, his right hand had lines of blood on it.

"The fuck is your problem?" He asked, holding his hand.

"Just... just... I'm not ready."

He looked like he was about to attack her, but then the fury in his eyes, along with the red glow, faded.

Everything seemed to deflate from him as he sunk to the ground beside her and started picking glass from his hand. He winced with each piece but kept on without a complaint.

She turned to watch several vampires that had created a fighting pit, taking drunken challengers on. The first two were soon thrown out, a new champion in their place, and more vampires stepped in to challenge. It was like roosters showing off for the hens, these semi-drunk vampires and their games.

Yet, she couldn't look away. It was like an old dance, a ritual among lovers and fighters, with the glow of flames shining on their sweaty bodies—many shirtless now—and she almost lost sight of the violence, instead seeing the flow of energy and the thrill of battle.

After watching at her side for a while, Brad asked, "You really think they're out there still?"

"What?"

"Your parents, I mean."

She wasn't sure how much he knew—she hadn't told him anything. Had he heard it from others? Her mother had talked in her sleep too... maybe now Robin was doing the same?"

"If they aren't..."

"Then what's the point?" He nodded. "Yeah, I get that."

"Your parents are out there too?" She lowered herself to his side, glad to see he had stopped picking at the glass.

His left lip turned up in a smile.

"Me? Not at all." At a concerned look from her, he added, "Oh, nothing to pity me for. Sure, I lost them early on, but I swore to myself I would survive. The point of life and all that? I couldn't give a shit. For me, it's just survival."

"And yet, you were caught up in all this."

He laughed. "*And yet?* You didn't know, Robin? I came looking for them."

"You volunteered to become a vampire?"

He nodded.

The thought of him wandering the world in search of groups of vampires to join made her even more confused about how to think of him. Many didn't believe in vampires, but here was this guy who devoted his life to finding out if they were real, and then becoming one of them.

A look in his eyes told her he was going for a kiss again, so she acted preemptively.

She stood and pushed him back, then hissed, "Why the hell would you want to be one of... us?"

"I knew there was one way to survive—become one of the elites, the best of the best. None of those rat-fucking pricks out there can touch me now, no motherfucker will put his hands on me. If I had been a vampire when they found us..."

"Oh, God." She put a hand to her mouth, horrified at where her mind was going with the interpretation of what he had just conveyed. "I'm so sorry."

"My mom was already dead, and they were coming for me next. My dad… he fought to get to me, told them that he would do anything, anything. You should have seen the look in his eyes when they came at me with a knife."

Robin gasped, both hands to her mouth now. A tear at the edge of her eye.

Brad sighed. "I'll never forget that look… Nor the relief when he saw that they had cut the ropes instead of my neck."

He sat there for a moment, staring off at the flames.

"Did… he make it?" she asked, hesitantly.

With a trembling lip, he shook his head. "They told me to fight for his life, that if I could take their guy, my dad would live. If I lost, it'd be his life and I could go. But I swear to God, all the fucking gods ever throughout any religion, I gave it everything." He clenched his teeth, breathing quickly through his nose. "It wasn't enough."

"I—I didn't know." She put an arm around him, and he leaned into her.

"It wasn't enough," he repeated, and then stood and, without looking back, walked over to the fighting pit. He leaped in, yelling for the next challenger, and two vampires turned on him.

They didn't stand a chance and had to be dragged out of there.

Again he shouted for more, but Giuseppe motioned to a couple of the experienced vampires, and together they were able to pull him out.

"That's enough for tonight," Giuseppe said when everyone had quieted and only Brad's shouts of "I can take you all!" could be heard. "Pack up, grab supplies. We're heading back before sunrise."

They went about it and soon were moving out. Brad stepped out from the crowd and gave her a shrug.

"Does 'sorry' work in this kind of situation?" he asked.

"Sorry for what?"

"Losing it. Being a bit of a tool. Anything else you can think of."

She took his arm, wrapping hers in it, and walked at his side. "You opened up to me, I appreciate that. Just… maybe try and keep your cool next time."

He laughed. "You can count on it."

"This world is a bit fucked, right?"

"A bit is a bit of an understatement, so let's say a bit here means totally and irreconcilably."

"You think we're so screwed?" She frowned, thinking back to what she had heard about the early days after the fall of civilization. They had come so far, but there was still so far left to go.

He nodded. "Human nature is evil in itself. Add to that vampires and Weres and what happens? Do regular humans join together to stop evil? No, they cower in fear and get wiped out—"

"Brad?"

"Yeah?" He looked at her, eyes wild, and then laughed. "Sorry, doing it again?"

"You were getting a *bit* carried away."

He laughed. "Irreconcilably carried away. That sounds about right."

BAM!

A shot came from ahead, and then three more. The vampires scattered into the trees, leaving their packs where they were. Soon more sounds of gunshots rang out, and then the screams of men being taken down by vampires.

Brad unslung his AK-47 and Robin drew her pistol. Her eyes searched the tree line, registering quick movements and men in military cammo.

"Local wannabe badasses," Brad said.

He was about to run off to help in what was bound to be a slaughter, when Robin clutched tighter to his arm.

Instead of protesting, he looked into her eyes, considered his options, and then nodded.

Even when the two saw a man running off on his own, Brad stayed at her side, though she could tell he was itching to run after the attacker and finish it.

"Let him go," Giuseppe said, stumbling into the bit of clearing where they were. He apparently thought they were debating whether to pursue or not. "I want them to know we're coming, so their pants are all soiled by pissing themselves by the time we arrive."

Robin simply shivered, once again reminded why she would have to find a way to leave these creatures behind. Where Brad fit into that picture, she had no idea.

CHAPTER FOURTEEN

Old Manhattan Docks

Royland and Cammie had been casing out the docks for most of the night, teetering on the point between exhaustion and just wanting to give up, when Cammie's ears perked up.

She recognized that voice.

Slowly, she crept to the side of a shipping crate and poked her head around it, then quickly pulled back.

"It's her," she whispered to Royland.

He snuck up next to her, pressing up almost against her body as he leaned out to have a look. His scent, like oak and iron, pulled at her and in spite of the odd coupling, made her want more.

"Did you just sniff me?" he asked.

"Barely perceptively," she replied, biting her lower lip.

"Maybe to a regular human." He pointed at his teeth and let his fangs show. "Vampire."

She could feel herself blushing again, the heat rising to her cheeks, and hated it. Why did she lose herself around this vampire? Thinking back to their sparring in the underground hideout, before they had made their move on Enforcer HQ, she remembered. The way he hadn't been afraid to hold back against her, knowing she could hold her own, made her see what kind of man he was.

While she was always flirtatious, she was the first to admit, it rarely meant anything. But with this guy?

She licked her lips and pulled him in for a quick kiss. He stared at her wide-eyed, and chuckled.

"Didn't we talk about me making the first move?"

"Not my style," she said with a shrug, then nodded over her shoulder. "What do we do about *traitor girl* over there?"

He frowned. "You kiss me out of the blue, and then change the subject like that?"

She smiled seductively. "We can keep going, but then she might escape."

Royland just shook his head. "You… either have problems, or are really amazing. I'm still trying to decide which. Probably a little of both. Now, can we focus?"

"Your loss," she said, and then moved around the shipping crate before she could see his reaction. Part of all this was just in good fun, but she actually liked this guy, and was starting to worry that her brash nature might scare him off.

Focus, she told herself as she crouch-walked toward where they had spotted Ella.

"That's not good enough," Ella said, and Cammie ducked down beside a stairwell, close enough to hear but stay out of sight.

"I can get you to the border of Old Portugal," a man said. "For what you're paying, no farther."

Cammie and Royland shared a look. This wasn't what they expected at all. With a shrug, Cammie stood.

"Portugal, Ella?" she said.

Ella and Peterson froze, hands on holsters, but didn't draw. The man they were talking with, a tall man with a long, leather jacket and a captain's hat typical of those sailing the blimps, took a step back, hands up.

"I don't need any trouble on this trip," he said. "You promised extra protection, not danger."

"It's fine," Ella said, taking her hand away from her pistol and motioning for Peterson to do the same. "Give us a minute."

The captain nodded, but only stepped back a few feet before stopping to wait. Cammie ignored him, approaching Ella.

"All of this was just to run away?" Cammie asked.

Ella's eyes darted between Cammie and Royland, and where there was usually defiance, now she seemed nervous. It was a weird emotion to see from her.

"We're fed up," Ella said. "All of this back and forth, it's too much. And even if we wanted to settle in, be part of the community now, we don't support it. But we're done fighting, so please, just pretend you didn't see us."

"You're not planning some crazy scheme, joining up with pirates or something?" Royland asked.

"Pirates?" the captain asked, leaning back into the conversation.

"No!" Ella looked to him, pleadingly. "We have nothing to do with pirates, I swear." She turned back to Cammie and Royland, hands out. "Just let us go. It's over right? I heard that Morgan called for peace, and I'm sure once that meeting's over, everyone will be happy, everything back as it was."

"The meeting's over." Cammie sniffed, then cleared her throat. "Everything is as you say."

"See? No hard feelings, nothing to worry about. In the end, it all works out!"

Cammie's mind flashed back to the Weres around her in the warehouse, raining down destruction on Morgan and her followers. The thought sent a shiver down her spine, but she nodded.

"Go," Cammie said.

"What?" Royland stepped close and leaned in to whisper. "Does that sound like justice to you?"

"Valerie isn't here. She put us in charge, and if our idea of right and wrong doesn't always gel with hers, well, that's part of what delegation is all about, right? Trusting those below you to make the correct choice. Not always the one you would have made."

"I'll point out that Valerie didn't kill Ella when she could have," Peterson said, speaking up for the first time since being caught. "And, I've always been a model cop. If you can't stand by me vouching for my sister, then it would be hopeless. But here I am, and Cammie has made her call. Do you agree, Royland?"

They all turned to the vampire, awaiting his decision. After a moment's thought, he nodded, and then turned to the captain and added, "See that they reach their destination."

"Thank you," Ella said.

Everyone turned to the captain, who harrumphed and then shook his head. "The shit I put up with in this town. I'm getting too old for it."

He walked off with a nod to Ella and Peterson.

Ella turned to Cammie and seemed unsure what to say, so Cammie held up a hand and said, "Just go."

Peterson nodded and the two walked off, following the captain, leaving Cammie and Royland by themselves. She ran a hand through her hair, noticing how oily it was and how much she would love to have a nice, long shower right now. Preferably, not by herself.

A quick glance at Royland made her smile, but then she remembered what he had said about making the move.

She nodded to the old port boarding zone, where some benches still remained from the old days, and took a seat.

"I'm beat," she said.

"Too beat for maybe… stopping by the café for a night cap?" He sat beside her and noticing her hand placed conveniently for him to see, took it in his.

Her well-timed yawn added to the effect when she put her other hand on his and gently caressed it. "I'm a bit tired for going out."

His eyes flitted down to her back, across her body, and up to her hopeful eyes. "I suppose, I mean… I did buy one of Sandra's bottles of wine, and I do have it in my room."

"If you promise to behave yourself," she said, doing her best not to laugh. The result, judging by the longing in his eyes, was more of a seductive smile.

He stood and held out his arm for her to take.

Always best to let the guy *think* he is in charge, she thought to herself. She wrapped her arm in his and followed him back to what, she would be sure was a night that, would make her forget all the unpleasantries of the day.

Presley and Esmerelda were going to miss out, but Cammie supposed she didn't have to share everything, at least for now. Maybe later if she wanted to spice things up, she'd invite them in, see if the vampire could handle it.

She giggled to herself.

"Everything okay?" he asked.

She leaned her head against his shoulder. "Perfect."

CHAPTER FIFTEEN

Unknown City

The moonlight lit up the city which was mostly in ruins, but as Valerie and her companions approached, they spotted several residential neighborhoods in fairly good condition, and in the city itself there were several tall, window-covered buildings still standing.

The most interesting, though, was a large building with marble stairs and columns, straight out of the old days, Valerie imagined. This would have been either a museum or where government officials conducted their business.

And at the moment, she could tell by the sudden shift in the winds, it was occupied by a vampire—a Forsaken.

She first saw him standing on the roof, looking away from them, but he must have sensed her, because he turned just as she looked up.

They locked eyes for a moment, and then he made a signal by raising his right arm and then extending it toward them.

"What the hell's that about?" Diego asked.

His answer came in the form of what sounded like a war cry and the pounding of feet on concrete.

"There!" Valerie shouted, pointing to the nearest shelter, one of the glass buildings. "Get out of sight."

The other two ran for it, but not her. She was already going the other way, hoping that she could distract the wild horde of people she now saw rounding the marble building. They were all barefoot and mostly nude but for loincloths for the men and what looked like potato sacks for the women.

Running fast enough to outpace them but not so fast as to lose them, she made for the marble building and the Forsaken. If he didn't have any other information, he might at least be able to tell her where they were, once she forced it out of him.

Even as she reached the first marble column and used it to jump and push off to reach the first window's ledge, she could feel the cold aura coming from the Forsaken above. Cold and something else. Sharp? He was already afraid.

And if he was afraid, that meant she just had to push it a tad further. She leaped up and pushed out with the fear hard, as she grabbed onto the next ledge and chicken-winged herself up.

By the time she reached the roof, she could feel the cold aura had melted into a slight chill, pulsating from him, and the words, "Who are you?" floated through the air like wisps of clouds.

She grasped onto it, smiling, and said, "I'm no one to be trifled with."

He tilted his head. "Did… you just quote a movie?"

"A what?"

In spite of the terror in his eyes, the Forsaken laughed and shook his head. "Nothing. Something from the old days."

"Call them off!" she demanded. There wasn't time for this cryptic bullshit. "Now!"

He stumbled back as she pushed with the fear again, the smile vanishing instantly.

But he stood, defiantly. "Who are you? How—how did you do that? And you arrived without any sort of protective clothing." He sniffed the air and nodded to himself. "Yes, there's no doubt, you're a vampire. And since you seem to have walked here… A day-walking vampire?"

"Call. Them. Off."

She stepped forward, mere feet away, and pulled her sword.

"Yes, yes, of course." He stood, went to the edge of the roof, and waved an arm as he shouted, "Stand down."

Immediately the command was repeated throughout the crowd, and they all froze in place, then turned to face him.

"You see," he said, glancing over his shoulder at her, "you're not the only one here with power. Mine just comes in a different form."

"They're your slaves?"

"My followers, by choice. I led them to freedom, now they follow me."

"I have a hard time believing that."

He shrugged. "Believe what you will, but I'll tell you this. There are people, and there are other vampires, both of whom would enslave others to get ahead in life. I do what I can to ensure that doesn't happen."

"Let's say I believe you, or that I'm at least playing along." She went to the edge of the roof and used her vampire sight to look for Sandra and Diego, spotting them up a stairway on the side of a building. They were surrounded by this Forsaken's warriors. Sandra gave her a meek wave. "Why'd you attack us?"

"For all I know, you're one of these slavers. Rather, for all I knew, I should say. If they have a day-walking vampire among them who can do what you just did, I might as well surrender now, eh?"

"Eh? You from Canada?"

"I was, once."

She rubbed her chin in thought, then remembered why they were here. "I don't suppose we're close to Chicago?"

He laughed. "Far as I know, it's still a ways West. But you don't want to go there. Some big shot and his military followers. Call themselves the Force de Guerre, force of war, I believe it means. And they can be… lacking in forgiveness, from what I hear."

"Intolerant of injustice, from what *I* hear." Valerie glanced back down at her friends, then said, "We'll be on our way. You try to stop us, I'll kill you."

"See, there's our problem," he said. "I have your friends surrounded, and can have them killed with a wave of my hand. Seeing as you know where we are, and are super powerful, but… given that I know nothing of you, I'm not sure just letting you go is such a good idea."

"Okay, now you listen here," in a split-second she had him by the neck, lifting him off the ground. "I could squeeze right now and watch your head pop right off like a pea from its pod. You threaten me or my friends again, well… let's just say I like peas." She stared into his eyes, allowing hers to glow red and the fear to push out again, then added, "Yum."

He looked like he was about to piss himself, and then started laughing.

She squeezed, cocking her head in confusion.

"Ack," he held up his hands in surrender. "No, no, I'm sorry. It was a test, see? If you didn't care about your friends, that's how I'd know you were one of them. They have no loyalty, not the ones who are knee deep in it."

Lowering him, she returned her eyes to normal, but didn't loosen the grip. "A test? You want to test me? How about the fact that I didn't kill you, but could've many times over."

"That and the *I'm no one to be trifled with* line," he said, his voice almost mocking her, she was certain, "yeah, I was already leaning toward trusting you anyway."

"And how do we know we can trust you?"

He grinned, then shrugged. "Ask my people. Have I done bad things in my time as a vampire? Certainly. But in this new world, I've found a new calling, a new way of living. A community."

"Fine. We need rest anyway, some real food, if you have any to spare. Some clean water, maybe?"

He nodded and motioned to the city around him. "Welcome, my lady, to Cleveland, Ohio."

He had introduced himself as Gerald, and soon they were all acquainted. The strange Ohioans and the Forsaken sat around campfires as the vampire told them stories of the old days, of his travels, and more specifically, of his time with the slavers.

Valerie nodded, taking special interest in the subject. First her brother, then vampire hunters and bleeders, and now this? America had a long way to go still. It made her head swim, just thinking about all the work she had to do.

But as Michael's Justice Enforcer, she intended to do everything she could.

"What do they do with the slaves, though?" Sandra asked, her voice shaking. Valerie had almost forgotten that the woman had once, effectively, been her slave.

"Sometimes they use them to simply serve, others, it's unspeakable," Gerald said, staring off into the fire. "One time, I found a woman being used as target practice with knives."

"Damn," Valerie said. It didn't necessarily surprise her, after being involved with Donovan, but that didn't mean it was easy to hear.

"That was the night I betrayed my kind." Gerald lifted a stick and stirred the embers of their fire.

"You couldn't stand to be around them after that?" Diego asked.

Gerald chuckled. "Not exactly. They were trying to kill me, see, after I rescued the woman and tore off the head of the vampire who was hurting her."

"That'll do it."

Valerie nodded. "Good for you." She was smiling, but the smile suddenly vanished as she had a realization. "And the woman…?"

He shook his head. "They got her. I tried to feed her from my blood, to stop it, heal her. Even tried to make her a vampire… but it was too late."

A moment of silence followed, but Valerie had to know.

"Did… did you ever avenge her?"

He looked up at her over the fire. "The one who did it? Yes, but the rest of them are still out there. I wouldn't stand a chance against them, so I settled down here with the plan of helping as many people as I could to never suffer like she did."

"And we'd follow you to our deaths, if you asked for it," a heavyset man with bloodshot eyes said from across the fire. His dark beard was long enough to make up for the lack of hair on his head. "You ever say the word, you know we will."

"I know this, Amos."

The others around the table chorused their agreements, and Valerie was impressed with the loyalty and admiration in their eyes.

"There was a time," she said, "when I thought I was the only good vampire in the world. Can you believe it? But you'll be happy to hear, if you think like I did, you're not."

He seemed to be unsure, but nodded.

"You ever come to Old Manhattan, you'll see I speak the truth," she said. "And there's a couple more roaming about, who you'd probably find somewhere in Europe, at this point."

"I might take you up on that." Gerald looked around at his followers, eyes coming to rest on Amos. "But even if everyone here would follow me, I can't ask that of you all. This is your home."

"It's your home too, now," Amos said.

Gerald nodded, then turned back to Valerie. "He's right. But you and yours will be welcome whenever you come through this area."

"And if I ever come calling, in need of every man and vampire I can find to stand up and fight alongside me and mine?"

"That would have to be a mighty important mission."

Sandra cocked her head and mouthed, "What are you talking about?"

"Thing is," Valerie added, "I don't like the stories like the one you shared with me, about this woman you loved. I don't like them one bit, and when I'm done here, I plan on having a united America, a land where, even if we're divided by wastelands and ruined cities, the cities that remain will be safe-havens where anyone is welcome, as long as they pursue a life filled with honor. Do you share this dream of mine?"

Gerald laughed. "You have big dreams, that's for sure. But you know, sitting here with you and listening to the way you say it, I believe you might indeed be the one to see it through. Should that day ever come, you can count on me."

"On all of us," Amos said. He clapped the woman's shoulder

to his right. "Ain't that right?"

She crossed her heart with her fist and bowed her head briefly, before smiling and saying, "Damn straight. But I got one question," she winked at Valerie as she said the next part, then nodded at Diego. "What's the story with this one?"

"What do you mean, what's my story?" Diego said. "I was born—"

"No, no, no." She held a finger to his lips, and Amos laughed. "What I meant was, how interested are you in members of the opposite sex, particularly, the one talking to you right now."

"Wow, if that was a proposition," Sandra scooted closer to Diego, putting an arm around him, "you've got to work on your style. Also, he's spoken for."

Amos grinned at the woman and said, "You getting lonely, you know I'm always up for it."

She froze, turned and socked him across the jaw, and then walked off.

Valerie had sat up straight at that, but relaxed when she saw that Gerald was smiling.

"It's been like that for about a month," he said. "Ever since the dick cheated on her."

Amos rubbed his jaw and shrugged. "I'm an idiot. What can I say?"

"You can say 'I'll never sleep with your sister again,' and see if that makes a difference," Gerald said.

"True, sure," Amos said. "But then again, I've been raised to never lie."

"Cheating is fine, but lying isn't?" Sandra asked, glaring.

"Hey, I never said my parents were perfect, far from it." He chuckled, staring off at the stars. "Just said that's how I was raised, didn't I?"

“Tell you what, Amos,” Valerie said, leaning forward so that she felt the heat of the flames dancing on her cheeks. “You ever want to fight alongside me, I’ll treasure that day. But no way in hell will I ever let you get close to any of my girlfriends.”

“I take it you’re taken then?”

“Know when to turn it off,” she said, and the others laughed at him as he leaned back and shrugged.

“You’re not technically taken at the moment,” Sandra said, much to Valerie’s annoyance. “I mean, you two are kind of on a break, right? At least until you know what’s the deal out here and when we’re going back?”

Valerie shot Sandra a glare. “Shut up, will you?”

Sandra laughed and motioned zipping her lips.

“And, for your information, I’m not like this slut-guy here,” Valerie added. “So, let’s just not discuss my love life with strangers, even if they are pretty cool strangers at that?”

“Deal.”

“Many people will be resting soon,” Gerald said. “You all are welcome to sleep here and get back to your journey in the morning.”

“Offer accepted,” Valerie said with a grin.

They stayed up a bit longer, sharing stories of what had happened in Old Manhattan and receiving stories of the surrounding areas where these people had come from. Some had faced horrors at the hands of Forsaken, but many had never come across a vampire or any member of the UnknownWorld before meeting Gerald.

It was clear he had a bit of a cult following—some seeing him at first as some sort of god, but as he had shown them more and more of his true self, they had come to see the man in him, and the leader.

As Valerie closed her eyes that night, with Diego taking the first watch, she thought about a world where people worshiped vampires, and what a horrible world that would be. Sure, she had taken a turn for the better, but she didn't know a single vampire, werewolf, or regular human that was worthy of worship. The whole idea felt so wrong.

When she finished setting this land straight, telling them the whole truth about her kind might be something she would have to consider. Perhaps the old ways of keeping the UnknownWorld hidden was no longer relevant, especially when the alternative to being open and honest meant humans worshiping vampires.

Halfway through the night, Diego woke her for her shift, and she stood vigil, considering the stories this vampire had told her. She had already heard too many bad things about vampires up north among the pirates, and now one of their own had confirmed those stories firsthand.

Some of the local groups he had referred to might be just as capable of atrocities, and she knew the Black Plague certainly was.

At some point, she would have to see this land healed.

When morning came without problems, the trio bade their hosts goodbye and packed up their belongings, along with fresh food that Gerald's group had been able to part with. Even Valerie had to admit, it hadn't been a bad side-trip.

CHAPTER SIXTEEN

Black Plague HQ

Robin stood before her new team—freshly made vampires assigned to her as a test, ready to begin their training.

Brad smiled at her, his own new recruits standing before him, and she smiled back. Whatever they had been through, this was the next phase. They were to train these vampires to be warriors, assassins capable of moving in to take over, first Chicago, and then expand. With the funding from some men known as the CEOs, they were going to conquer the world, or so they were told.

She, for her part, still had every intention of running when the moment was right. When that would be, however, she had no clue. First of all, they couldn't survive in the sunlight. That was no myth. It had proven to be true.

Perhaps she could snag some of the protective clothing the vampires had worn when they went off to attack Valerie, and also the tents they used. All that gear would be heavy though, and while she was strong now, she really had no clue which way to go or how long she would be able to last on her own.

Another glance at Brad, and she wondered about his allegiances here. Would he possibly get interested in accompanying her? Helping her across the Fallen Lands to search out her family?

He had already started showing his recruits the basic fighting stance, a blade flashing in his hand as he explained a means of attack. Even if he was nice to her at times, the look in his eyes as he trained them gave her a bad feeling. He was one of them now, fully indoctrinated.

Giuseppe walked by and cleared his throat, pulling her back from her thoughts.

"Everything fine, Robin?" he asked.

She nodded curtly and then turned to address her recruits.

However, a murmur arose from those close to the courtyard entrance, and several groups ran over. With a shared look of curiosity between her and Giuseppe, she motioned to her recruits and they all ran over, together.

Barely visible in the moonlight, they could make out a figure approaching, fast.

"One of ours," Giuseppe said, squinting. "This can't be good."

A moment later the vampire was among them, shouting for them to get out of the way.

"Leon," Giuseppe called out. "What is it?"

The vampire, Leon, paused to stare at him, his eyes wide with confusion, as if he almost didn't know where he was. His clothes were tattered, blood running down his chin. He must have fed to make it here so fast.

"The other two, are gone," he said, collapsing to his knees.

"And the vampire princess?" Giuseppe said. "The one they call Valerie?"

A look of interest crept over Leon's face, a slight smile, and he said, "Dead. She's dead," and then fell face forward in the dirt, unconscious.

"Get this man to his room," Giuseppe ordered two vampires nearby. "The elders will need to see him, maybe even… yes. Just, get a move on it."

When he turned back to Robin, his eyes were wild with excitement.

"What does this mean for us?" Robin asked.

"For us?" He laughed. "It means war. It means that as soon as we take Chicago, we'll make our move on New York. The vampire princess is no longer there to stop us."

◈ ◈ ◈

Fallen Lands

Valerie, Diego, and Sandra wondered how long the journey could last, each of them growing sick of it.

They had entered a rocky area, full of rubble from the ruins of old houses, with a strong scent of earth in the air. A quarry was on their left, and soon they were passing it, staying low and out of sight in case anyone was around.

A low holler sounded, and they ducked behind a five-foot drop-off as several wild looking men and woman in bear and wolf hides ran past, some freshly killed vermin in their hands.

Diego's fists were clenching and unclenching, and Valerie

was pretty sure she knew why.

"More likely than not, they weren't Weres," Valerie said, trying to comfort him but barely able to hide the fury from her own voice. "And we can't be going around picking fights with people for no reason."

"Plus, we might want to hurry," Sandra said, pointing to the sky to the south. There were thick clouds, gray at the edges, bursting with blue flashes of lightning. "If we can avoid that storm, that would be a win in my book."

Diego nodded, though still glanced back with clenched fists as they left the quarry behind.

They were an hour gone before the winds caught them. Strong winds pulled leaves and dust from the ground and threw it at them one moment, sent it spiraling the next. A line of trees ahead creaked against the force, but provided shelter when the rains started. It got worse when any of them had to relieve themselves and couldn't be sure which way the wind would blow from one minute to the next.

But they pushed on, soon the storm was over and they were able to find semi-dry clothes in their packs.

The trees here were dense, but allowed them enough openings to watch the sun reach its peak overhead and then begin its descent.

Valerie came to a stop where the trees gave way, only then realizing it was to a drop-off beyond. While her first thought was to figure out a way down, the moment her eyes lifted to the land below she could only think one word – *finally*.

Down there, past several rolling hills, green from where vegetation had overtaken old suburban ruins, past a river, and farther still, she saw the lakes and what she had to assume was Chicago.

"Hurry your asses," she said with a cocky smirk to Sandra and Diego.

Diego was the first to reach the spot, and his wary expression suddenly brightened, as if he'd just had a four-course dinner ending with steak and a glass of Sandra's wine.

"Don't tell me…" Sandra said, her voice thick with annoyance.

But she stopped and just stared.

"Aren't you going to say anything?" Valerie asked.

Sandra pursed her lips, considering, then said, "I'm still trying to decide if it's real, or just a hallucination.

"It's real."

"A mirage then?"

"It's. Fucking. Real." Valerie looked to Diego for help.

He just shrugged and said, "Hey, I'm as happy as a bull on stampede day."

Sandra and Valerie both turned to look at him.

"What? Don't tell me you don't know what that is?" He looked at them like they were crazy. "Come on, when… oh, right, France. What did the leadership do there for public punishments?"

Sandra frowned. "You're telling me that in Spain, they would put people in a pen and let a bull go after them… for punishment?"

"Hell, you wouldn't think about stealing again after watching your brother go through that, right?"

"No, but I'd sure consider ways to kill the bastard who was making people do that in the first place."

"You'd have to kill him again," Valerie said, "because I'd already have killed him."

"Someone else would just pop up in their place." Diego shrugged. "After a while, you stop worrying about it, because you don't want to risk getting someone even worse and more corrupt than what you've got."

Valerie sighed. "Well, I'll just say I'm glad New York isn't like that now. Cammie, Royland, Donnoly, they're all great."

"And Jackson too," Diego said, before realizing both ladies were glaring at him. "What?"

Sandra hit him, and Valerie just turned back to the city in the distance.

"Don't worry about it," she said, and then worked her way off to a find a way down the hill.

They zigzagged down, sometimes having to grab roots or secure rocks to lower themselves down over a steep section, but soon they had reached the bottom. From there it was all straight walking, aside from the river, which was easy enough—a section of it was narrow, with white, glistening rocks close enough that they could leap between them to get across.

The sun was approaching the lakes to the west now, casting a shadow that reminded Valerie that, in spite of her joy at finally arriving, they hadn't come for merriment.

They were here to dole out justice.

CHAPTER SEVENTEEN

Enforcer HQ

Cammie couldn't get enough of Royland, and judging by the heavy panting and crazed look in his eyes as he looked up at her riding him, the feeling was mutual. With a final moan of ecstasy, she pressed her body against his and mimed biting his chest.

"I'm the vampire, here, don't forget," he said. "You're only supposed to bite when you're transformed."

"Ew, please tell me you're not into *that*." She rolled to his side, finger caressing his chest. "I have to draw the line somewhere."

"Into… oh, God no!" He laughed and gave her a fake shove. "Is this what you call sexy talk?"

"Hey, I was just being playful. You're the one who started imagining me as a wolf while—"

"Okay, okay, enough." He sat up and shook his head, as if that would clear the image from his mind. "We gotta get dressed before someone finds us here."

She laughed, looking around at the café's back room floor, where they lay. Yeah, not their finest hour, but since going back to his place, it was like they were unleashing everything built up between the two of them over the last couple of months.

"They're late, actually," she said. "I mean, we probably should've been interrupted about thirty minutes ago."

"I'm glad we weren't."

"You and me both, bub. Twice."

He grinned. "Vampire stamina."

That earned him another laugh. She stood to find her clothes and start dressing. Midway between fastening her bra, a knock came from the back door. The two shared a look of relief as she pulled on her shirt.

"Good timing," she said.

She tossed him his shirt, pausing to watch how the shadows maneuvered across his abs as he turned to put it on.

The knock came again.

"Coming, coming," Cammie said, then opened the door.

A man stood there with a cut across one cheek, his left hand pressing a cloth against his upper forearm, which seemed to be bleeding. He was short, but with thick arms and a strong chin that was covered in stubble.

With a grunt, he leaned against the doorway and said, "Shipment's not coming. Bloody pirates."

"You've got to be kidding me," Cammie said, the shock of it hitting her.

"Let him in," Royland said, nudging past her to wrap an arm around the man and help him sit. "Let me see the wound."

Cammie paced while he looked over the man. Each click

of her cowboy boots seemed to echo in the room, silent aside from the man's heavy breathing. There was a lot riding on this shipment, and the thought that someone else had just taken it really irked her.

"It's not bad," Royland said, "but we should get you stitched up to avoid scarring. If nothing else, get the wound cleaned."

"And how about the shipment?" Cammie demanded. "We can't recover from that."

Royland wiped his forehead in frustration, not realizing he had blood on his hand that now streaked across his face.

"We have to get it back," he said.

"Wait, what?"

"This problem is bigger than just some wine and cheese. There were munitions in there, and more. The medical supplies seized from the Bazaar will only last so long, and now with this… it's a matter of security and stability."

"Come with me." She walked into the main room, arms folded as she waited for him to join her.

"Sorry, just a sec," he said, his voice carrying out from the back room. He came over to her and looked like he wanted to take her hand, but seeing them in fists with the crossed arms, thought better of it.

"We have a duty here," Cammie hissed, doing her best to keep her voice low. "Valerie left *us* in charge."

"Us and Colonel Donnoly. He has Wallace, and we have our deputies. All I'm proposing is a scouting mission, initially. When we know where they take the goods, we come back here, round up a small army, and declare the days of pirating over."

"But—"

"But nothing." His voice was firm, strong, showing the

leader he was when in charge of his vampires. "Not only is it part of this City State's security, it's paramount to our survival."

"Still, I'd rather wait for Valerie to return."

"And you have some sort of idea when that would be?" He shook his head, knowingly. "The thing is, we don't have the luxury of waiting. What if another City State attacks, and we're low on supplies? Or someone who can't heal is cut open and we need those supplies? Or…"

"Or you don't have a bottle of wine to seduce me with next time," she said, playfully.

"I'll take that as capitulation?"

"No, you'll take it as me agreeing." She unfolded her arms and took his hand. "But just so you know, we might have to kill a lot of those sons of bitches."

"As much as I'm against it, anyone who stands between me and my tools of seduction probably deserves to die." His smile became a grimace. "Not really, but if they're threatening our security? Our lives? Then yes, we do what must be done."

"Well then, let's get this man to medical so we can set about making preparations for our trip."

He kissed her hand and said, "Our first vacation as a couple."

"We're a couple now?" she asked with a raised eyebrow.

"Yes." His tone held finality. No room for argument, and she liked it.

"Well then, sweet cheeks, let's get this show on the road. I've been wanting a vacation."

He rolled his eyes, but turned and walked away, giving her a playful sashay of his hips as he disappeared past the curtain into the back room.

While she was only joking about the vacation comment, she had to admit that the city had been making her feel claustrophobic lately. It always had, after being raised out in the Fallen Lands.

As much as this was going to be dangerous, possibly life-threatening, she was looking forward to it.

CHAPTER EIGHTEEN

Chicago Outskirts, Dusk

Gusts of wind carried the scent of meat grilling along with dust from years of unsettled dirt in the surrounding areas. Even Valerie had to shield her eyes—just because she could heal didn't mean her eyes had some sort of awesome repelling dirt function.

She would have to request that on the next upgrade, she thought with a smirk. There was a lot of dirt she would like to repel in this life.

A couple of large, cylindrical buildings stood sentry at the edge of town. As they approached, Valerie realized it could very well be a water treatment plant and a sewage plant. She could see why the CEOs would have chosen this as their fall-back point—better than the bandit camps with their sewage in the gutters, or even some of the other cities she imagined were out there struggling with how to get clean water. How many more people had died from diseases caused by dirty water and other inconveniences that they hadn't had to deal with before the great collapse?

As if fallout and the rest weren't enough to worry about.

They approached a worn-down bridge that crossed a narrow river, when the wind shifted and Valerie paused, eyes shifting. She held out a hand for the other two to stay still, then said, "We're not alone."

"Yes, Valerie," Diego said. "There's a whole city right there. Doesn't mean it's Chicago."

"Ye of little faith," Sandra said, standing tall, a smile on her face."

Valerie turned from the two and assessed it, wondering if they had finally found their destination. It was a vibrant city, well lit, and modern as modern went. Like Old Manhattan, Skyscrapers created a skyline that was a monument to the past, while the entire area was surrounded by dark ruins—well, except for the lakes.

"Come on," Valerie said. "Might as well find out."

They pushed on, their legs moving as if on their own, so used to this non-stop walking that had been their routine for a month now.

They came across a small stream, nothing like the river they'd crossed, though Diego slipped at the far side. His foot got wet, but nothing else. No harm done. It wasn't long before they were passing the treatment plants and could even make out some of the windows of the better-kept buildings of Chicago.

"I hope they have something better to eat than jerky and crackers," Diego said.

"What do you suppose the chances are that some of those blimps made it out this way with extra cheese?" Sandra said. "I mean, I never hoped they were holding out on me, but if it means they got some here, and it's waiting to be devoured by a true lover, I'm willing to look the other way this time.

"How about we deal with evil first, our cravings for cheese and steaks after?" Valerie asked, feeling the irritation creeping into her voice. She had brought several vials of blood, but hadn't wanted to use it all up on the journey over to feel her absolute best.

"Oh come on," Diego said. "I hadn't even thought about steaks! Ahhh, the thought of a thick, juicy, rib eye. Did I ever tell you about the steaks in Spain?"

"They have cows there?" Sandra asked, intrigued.

"One of the first things the new founder set up after the rebuilding started—farms on the outskirts of the cities. In Northern Spain, they know how to cook a mean steak. And I don't mean all red and cold in the center like you French."

"For your information, we don't do it that way," Sandra said. "In fact, we rarely eat steak at all, because the cows are so rare and then where would we get the cheese? So when we eat steak, it's only when they're close to death or when the meat's imported, and nowadays everyone's too paranoid about disease. So yeah, maybe before the collapse that was true, but—"

"Seriously, is this the time?" Valerie shot a brief frown his way, and then saw them—several people in camouflage, stepping out from the tall grass nearby. The group carried a variety of weapons, all except one, the youngest-looking of the group.

Valerie's instincts kicked in and she sniffed. One of them was special, Were special. The Were was attractive, but in that *do not mess with me* sort of way that most Weres had going on. A line of almost silver-white ran through her hair.

"That's close enough," a large soldier said, aiming in on

them and clearly eyeing Sandra's sniper rifle.

He glanced over his shoulder and said, "Where's the colonel?"

"He'll be along soon enough," the Were said, hands on her hips, assessing Valerie. She was tall, with sparkling purple eyes that studied the three, but especially Diego and Valerie, with interest.

"Please, just tell us," Sandra said, her voice full of exhaustion. "Is this Chicago?"

The Were nodded.

"Then that must make you part of this Force de Guerre we've heard so much about," Valerie said, keeping her voice level, not trying to intimidate or offend. "Keeping the peace?"

"Keeping the wrong outsiders out," the Were said. "When need be. Especially certain types of outsiders." Her eyes darted from Valerie and the sun at the edge of the hills, its rays casting long shadows across the ruins and trees.

"We're either welcome or we're not," Valerie said, not in the mood for games.

"I have to say, I'm curious," the Were said smoothly, tilting her head slightly and sniffing the air. "So yeah, welcome to Chicago. There's someone who'd like to meet you."

"Thanks, Char," a man's voice came from the tree line, and then he stepped out, rifle slung over his shoulder. "Is she…?"

"She is," the Were, Char, replied. "And the small one's a Were."

"That so?" The man looked impressed, then said, "I take it you're not with the Black Plague then?"

Valerie shook her head. "Though we do mean to stop them, so if you have any affiliation, better let us know sooner rather than later."

The soldier looked at her, then to the man. "What'ya say, Colonel?"

"I don't think we have new recruits for the Force de Guerre, TH," Char said.

Terry nodded. "That's true enough. But… one has to wonder what a day-walking vampire's doing around these parts?"

A moment of unease followed between Valerie and her companions.

"Maybe we should join them?" Sandra said. "I mean, can't hurt, right?"

Valerie pursed her lips, debating, and felt their thoughts, like a warm cup of tea, with a bit of spice. She still wasn't sure how to interpret these sensations, not exactly, but she figured that couldn't be all bad. Perhaps safe, but guarded.

"After introductions," Valerie said.

The man smiled and extended a hand. "Name's Terry Henry Walton. If you're here for the Black Plague, then we've got no quarrel with you."

She took the hand in a firm grip and smiled. "Valerie, and it's a pleasure, TH."

His eyes narrowed. "Let's go with Terry for now."

She nodded. "Thing is, Terry, we're here for more than just them. And I'd love to hear how much you know about this Black Plague group, but first, I think I better tell you everything."

He nodded, then motioned toward the outpost. "Inside, in case anyone's watching."

"Watching?" Sandra asked as they started walking.

Valerie gave the two a look that said, *proceed with caution.*

"We like to think we have this place under lockdown,"

TH said as he led the way. They walked past shrubs and around the bend of the outer perimeter of the city, where they saw a small outpost ahead. "But with the rumors of the Black Plague—"

"How much do you know of them?" Valerie asked and, judging by the look he gave her, he wasn't accustomed to being interrupted.

"Truthfully, not much." He reached the outpost and held the door open for the rest, following behind a moment later.

It was dark in here, except for the light from glass-less windows.

"First, I want to know what a vampire is doing walking around in the daylight," he said. "Second, whether you know where Akio is now."

"You assume he gave me the power?"

Terry nodded curtly.

"I can tell you where he is, but it wasn't him. He went to Europe, in pursuit of Michael."

"No…" Char said, stepping forward and staring into Valerie's eyes as if that would tell her if this was the truth. "Michael has returned?"

"He has. And Akio and Yuko just missed him. He was going off to France, to deal with some, er, unsavory characters."

Char and TH shared a look of excitement. TH took a big breath, and then looked at her with a new level of respect.

"We don't get many visitors here," he said. "Nor welcome them. But if what you say is true, if you actually knew Akio and mean to go after the Black Plague, you can stay as long as you need."

Char put a hand on his arm. "She did say they came for another reason."

"That's right, you did." He furrowed his brow and stood, waiting.

Valerie leaned back against a wooden beam, arms crossed, and said, "Better get comfortable, this could take a while." She went into the full story, about coming across the Ocean and finding out about the fact that people were hunting vampires for their blood, and how she had realized the problem came from the top, that to stop it she'd had to cut off the beast's head, leaving Old New York in a state of flux.

"A bit too trusting, I think," Char said. "You tell everyone you meet on the road your life story, you might want to watch out."

"People have certainly criticized me for being too trusting in the past," Valerie said. "Thing is, I figure it's better to trust and have people at your side, than to not trust and stand all alone. Plus, if anyone ever betrays me, I can remove their head from their body easily enough."

"Is that a threat?"

"It wasn't directed at anyone here." Valerie unfolded her arms and held her hands out, so she could show she meant no aggression. "More a statement of fact. There aren't many that could survive once I've decided they shouldn't."

"I believe her." Terry Henry Walton leaned back, hand on his pistol, assessing them through narrowed eyes. Finally, he raised an eyebrow and said, "Okay, here it is. We don't interfere with people if they come to us and say they want to be part of our society. These CEOs you speak of, we don't know if they're here or not, but do know that one man arrived recently with a pretty big posse. The type you watch out for, because they look like some mean mother fuckers, and because a group that size can always be trouble."

"If he's here, he is trouble."

Terry held up a hand. "If he is what you say, if he's done what you say he's done, I'd have to agree. So here's what we'll do. Extraction. You go in, you get him out, then you deal with him as you see fit. But you cause a scene, you make trouble in Chicago, then we've got ourselves a problem, you and me."

She didn't know this guy, but she sensed something different about him—he didn't have the Were or vampire scent, but… there was something. That, plus the look in his eye, was enough to decide she'd trust him about this.

"You have yourself a deal," she said.

"Oh, and Sergeant Garcia is going with you," Terry said, pointing to a man leaning against a wall, He looked one hundred percent military from his uniform, to the short hair, to the weapons he carried. The kind of man Valerie associated with Commander Strake and the Enforcers, she thought, instantly distrusting him.

"I work best with my team, no one else." Valerie stood tall now, staring him down.

"This is our city. Would you let outsiders enter your city fully armed without an escort?" He assessed her, then shook his head. "I didn't think so. It's set then."

"Deal," she said, shaking his hand.

Terry ran a hand through his hair and raised an eyebrow. "You've got a big mission ahead of you. Best get to it."

CHAPTER NINETEEN

Outside Chicago

Robin had been shaking uncontrollably when she took that first step into the light of pre-dusk. She expected to explode or burst into flames or something, unable to fully accept that the protective clothing and facemask she put on would protect her or the others.

However, they had walked into the light, heads down, eyes covered, and were soon making their way out toward their destination: Chicago.

The mission was to scout it out, prepare for the attack. They would take out the guards, then, when all was ready, send the message that it was time to send in the army. Since they only had a limited number of protective outfits, the rest would remain at Black Plague HQ until sunset waiting to receive the word that it was time.

Long shadows formed behind even the smallest pebbles—something Robin had never paid attention to in the past. When she once dared to glance up, the angle of the sun was too much and burned even through her protective lenses, so she ducked her head and continued on like the rest.

She had to laugh at the thought of anyone watching them. What would they think when they saw a dozen people all in black, walking without looking up? Maybe they would assume it was some strange mourning ritual for the dead.

In a way, it kind of was.

"How far is this place?" Brad asked from his position beside her.

"Not a clue," she said, shaking her head. "But I don't know why we couldn't just wait for sunset."

"Probably because it's damn far away," he replied. "And we'll want to make it back before sunrise."

She nodded. That made sense, actually.

"Wake me when we get there?" he said, and she could hear the grin in his voice.

"Oh, you'll sleepwalk the rest of the way? Good! Some peace and quiet."

"Peace?" He laughed. "I think that's the last thing we'll be having tonight."

"How about the quiet part at least?" she said, more to distract herself from the sinking feeling in her stomach as they walked. Tonight would be different from the other nights, she imagined. If she didn't fight tonight, she might die. Brad might die.

But to fight, to kill, and live… She wasn't sure which would be worse. They trekked on and on, and past busted pipes sticking out of the ground, nasty smelling old sewage facilities no longer in use, and buses toppled over and covered in overgrowth.

Soon that horrible orb of death known as the sun

descended behind the ruins and wastelands to the west, and the stars began to sparkle overhead. The vampires were able to remove the protective clothing and goggles.

A breath of fresh air felt amazing.

"Not much farther," the lead vampire said, and before long they saw the lights of the city in the distance.

It was like nothing Robin remembered ever seeing. She had been raised mostly on the move, staying for a while occasionally in settlements, sometimes with generators that provided electricity. But nothing like what they saw now.

A voice sounded nearby, then a scent in the wind—vampire!

It wasn't one of theirs, Robin was sure of it. This one felt different, with a hint of sweet to it—like a mist of perfume caught in the wind. Then something else, something less appealing.

"What's that?" she asked, and Brad looked at her, knowingly.

"Were," he said, holding up a hand to get everyone's attention, then hissed, "Back, now!"

Everyone turned, pulling back twenty feet and finding cover.

"The hell's this about?" the lead vampire asked, running over while staying low to avoid being seen.

"If they smell us, our mission's blown," Brad said in explanation.

"The hell's a vampire and some Weres doing with them anyway?" the lead vampire asked.

"How do we know it's just one? They could have a whole army of vampires waiting for us."

"We have to get back and warn Giuseppe and the others," Robin said.

"Are you crazy? We have a mission!"

Robin turned on this vampire and was about to yell, but controlled herself, remembering that the strange vampire wasn't far off. "Did you even stop to think that this could be the vampire they were sending the others after, from New York? That maybe she's still alive, that the hit failed, and that this somehow ties into her coming after us for what we did?"

The others all stared at her, horrified.

"Shit, no," the lead vampire admitted. "We have to get back. Now."

Robin gave him an annoyed raise of her eyebrows, but he was already moving, passing the command on to the others. With another look back toward Chicago, she saw several silhouettes moving across the land, headed toward the city.

If this was the female devil they all spoke about, Robin couldn't let her win. Winning meant Robin's death, because she was one of these assassins now, effectively.

And if she died, that meant never finding out what had happened to her family, and, if they were still alive, not saving them.

Nobody was going to stand between her and her family. Not even this all-powerful bitch from hell.

CHAPTER TWENTY

Chicago

The lights had grown dim outside of Chicago, but the city was speckled with light pouring out from windows. It wasn't quite like Old Manhattan, given the lack of tall billboards and police pods, and the only sort of transit Valerie could spot was an old track that ran above their heads. She wasn't even sure it still worked, as the night was largely silent.

Valerie was impressed with the cleanliness of it all. She supposed that had to do with TH and his military ways. Contrasted with Commander Strake and his attitude of not caring, as long as he had order, she could see why that would be the case.

A gentle breeze blew from the northeast, carrying with it the scent of the trees they had trekked through to get here. She was so glad that was finally over.

Garcia led the way, waving off a couple of police who eyed

the strangers and stood guard outside of one of the mostly intact skyscrapers.

"You'll get more of that," Garcia said, motioning them into an alley behind the building, so they would be off of the main road. "These people have seen enough of the outside world to know that it isn't all sunshine and lollipops."

"But you have lollipops?" Sandra asked.

He glanced at her like she was stupid. "What? No, I don't even know what that means. It's just a saying."

"God, when bringing wine and cheese over, I hadn't even thought about lollipops," Sandra muttered to herself.

Valerie couldn't help but chuckle at the disappointment in Sandra's voice. Whatever the hell a lollipop was must have been very special.

Soon they came out behind a small building that looked to be a bar, judging by the large bottles and scent of beer. Several tall buildings rose up on the other side of a plaza, and Garcia pointed to them.

"The one on the left," he said. "That's where this outsider is staying. We've seen at least one, though two others have visited. They didn't stay long, and while they were here, there was arguing and a chair thrown from the window up top. It nearly took someone out.

"And security into there?" Valerie asked.

"This is where it gets complicated. Those boys are ours, not his. The FDG keeps the external peace, and you're external, so we trust you won't be harming them or we have a problem."

Sandra scoffed. "Do you really want a problem with a day-walking vampire who can take on your whole army by herself?"

The sergeant turned and glared, but Valerie waved them

both off. "Enough. The target is there, you say?"

Garcia nodded, not taking his glare from Sandra, who stood her own and glared back.

"Okay, while you two bat eyelashes and we test Diego's tolerance, I'm going to go ahead and kill this bastard."

She spun on her heels to go, but Sandra finally looked to her and said, "Wait."

"I'd rather not."

"We came all this way. What do you want us to do?"

Valerie cocked her head in thought, then nodded and said, "Cover me. If you see reinforcements coming, hold them off. If there's chaos, try to keep your people off me, Sergeant, and if I come running with attackers on my tail, snipe the hell out of them."

"You want us to just wait out here, basically?" Diego asked.

"It'll be cleaner this way. In and out."

Sandra furrowed her brow. "Fine, but… just try to keep him alive. He might know where others are."

"Dammit, why do you have to spoil my fun?" Valerie frowned, looking back up at the building. "Okay, so no killing guards, and no killing the target. This will make for a fun little excursion."

"When we first met, you weren't super into killing," Diego said. "Just get back into that mindset."

Garcia laughed. "A vampire *not* into killing? Now I have something to tell the grandkids someday."

"Actually, I'd still rather not take a life if the punishment isn't earned. The problem is that a lot of people have earned it."

"And you get to judge them? Why?"

"Have you heard of Michael?"

He frowned. "The Archangel?"

"The Dark Messiah returned. He granted me the power and authority, and I intend to use both, as appropriate."

"I don't know anything about this Dark Messiah, but I'll say this. One thing I've learned here with the colonel, life is precious. Don't take it lightly."

"Don't take life lightly, or don't take a life lightly?"

"Both."

She nodded. "I won't argue with that."

With a final nod and quick discussion to ensure everyone knew the plan, Valerie replaced her jacket with the sergeant's, though it was clearly too big, and then she placed his cap on her head. It gave her the look of one of them, almost. Then she turned to the building and started walking.

Along the way, she had to pull down her hat so that the heavy winds didn't blow it away, and she paused at the second building as if sheltering herself from the wind. In truth, she was assessing the guards at the building's base.

The plan had been to go up into the second building over and make it across from there, but now that she was standing here, she thought this might be easier than they had first thought.

Why kill anyone, when she could just as easily walk past them?

She took a small sip from one of her vials of blood and felt the boost to get her topped up. Garcia and the others hadn't accounted for her speed, since there was no way they could understand it.

She walked forward, casually, but keeping to the shadows, and then double-timed it before breaking into a vampire-speed sprint. The wind blew at that moment, or maybe it was a reaction to her speed, but either way the guards braced themselves against the chill and had no idea she had entered.

Inside was what had once been a grand reception area, but now appeared to be set up for more necessary operations. An image flashed in her mind of her reaching the rooftop of Enforcer HQ, only to find out she was too late. That wasn't about to happen here.

In and out, that was her mission here, so she turned to the stairs, ready to bound up them three or four at a time, when a hearty laugh sounded nearby.

Out of the corner of her eye, she saw a large man with a portly belly come walking around a corner, five guards in tow. He was smiling, and just started to turn her way when she ducked out of sight behind a desk.

"Just bring the pod around front," he told one of his guards. "They gave me an hour, I've already taken two."

"Had to get yours," one of the other guys said, and the big one laughed again.

"Ain't that the truth. Shit, the women in New York trailed far behind what you have here in Chicago."

"You'd think we import them, but nope. Mostly home-grown goodness."

"That's not what I hear," the large man said, who Valerie was starting to suspect was the CEO she'd come after. "Everyone knows about the slavers."

"We don't partake."

Valerie inched forward to have a better look. The group hovered around the door. Could the FDG have any idea this was going on under their very noses? She doubted it very much. Not TH, not with the way he ran his team, or how she expected anyway.

Then again, hadn't he or Garcia said something about keeping the place safe externally? She knew that the CEO didn't appear to be a threat on his own, but to let him and, presumably, the other two come and go seemed like a pretty big red flag to her.

The CEO grunted as a pod pulled up out front. It looked like one from Old Manhattan, black with reflective windows. When the doors opened, the CEO's guards moved out first, securing the area, and then he made his way out.

What to do? Valerie leaned forward, her mind racing. Sometimes she wished she could move her thoughts in vampire speed just like her legs, but it didn't work that way. She had planned to retrieve him, bind him, and carry him out of there. Damn, she bit her lip in frustration. Now that she thought about it, that wasn't much of a plan to begin with! She blamed her exhaustion from the long journey. TH and the others didn't care, as long as she didn't cause trouble or needless death, so… she might as well just take him.

Not wanting to waste any more time, she charged forward, pushing out with fear, hard. People in the building shrieked and a loud thump sounded from the floor above, and even the guards fell back, looking to the sky and then all around.

The CEO stumbled, but he was already at the pod and, before Valerie could reach him, he entered. She jumped in and was inside the pod a moment later, grabbing hold of him.

His eyes went wide and he shouted, "Go, go, go!"

The driver glanced back and his eyes went wide too, but Valerie kept hold of the man's collar. Suddenly she was thrown back as the pod lurched forward, then they were pulling away from the building, and the large man was struggling.

Of course, he was no match for her, but it was kind of annoying.

"Are you one of the CEOs of Old Manhattan?" Valerie shouted. "One of the Three Amigos?"

His eyes went wide, and he fell back into the seat as the pod settled.

The driver glanced back, confused, totally lost for what to do here.

"Pull over, there!" she said, indicating the bar where she knew her friends would be hiding nearby. They would have seen her jumping into the pod, she imagined. Unless they were still looking for her to stick with the original plan. "Not in the front, in the alley on the far side."

The guy looked about to protest, so she flashed red in her eyes.

"You're the she-devil," the CEO muttered, and then, to her surprise, he started to cry. It wasn't just a simple tear down the cheek sort of cry either, it was straight up bawling, his jowls shaking and blubber moving like a hippo caught in a net.

"The hell's he doing?" she asked the driver, who just looked between her and the CEO in utter bewilderment, then turned back to swerve and narrowly avoid the building before them.

Valerie squatted opposite the CEO and allowed her eyes to return to normal. She wasn't pushing fear anymore, because he was already about to piss himself.

"Your name?" she demanded. "Which one of them are you?"

"Don't, please don't hurt me," he pleaded.

"Give me a name, and we'll see."

"Ian, Ian Monzon."

"And the others?"

He whimpered, but said, "Dmitri Cross and Alex Manning."

"Not their names, where are they?"

The pod came to a rest and Valerie adjusted to glance back and ensure they weren't followed. So far, a peaceful night.

Ian was staring at her, the look in his eyes going from craven to insane man one moment to the next.

With a grunt, the insane man part won out and he lunged, saliva dripping down his chins and meaty hands reaching for her.

She rolled her eyes and slapped him, hard, so that he fell back into his seat and whimpered again. When he looked back up, it was clear he had lost the fight. Or was it something more than courage and cowardice?

"You're a schizo," she said, amazed. "I've heard talk of people like you, but… wow. My first real, live schizo."

"FUCK YOU!" Ian said, and she raised a hand to slap him again.

He pulled back, legs up and arms around his knees.

"If I can?" the driver said, turned around to watch. "He doesn't follow the exact patterns of a schizo, so, I don't know if that's entirely accurate. Insane is more like it."

Valerie nodded to the driver without turning her head, then considered the fat man before her. "Okay, well I can't very well execute an insane man, can I?"

She glanced back to the driver, who shrugged.

"I mean, justice is a bit murky on the subject, isn't it?" She held her chin in deep thought.

"I'll show you to them," Ian said. "You let me live, throw me in your prisons or whatever you need to do, but let me live, and I swear you'll have your justice." He leaned forward now, the tears still there, but a pure psycho dick-head look in his eyes. "I've always hated those rat-fucks anyway. Let me be the one that sticks 'em with the pointy end. Ooh, that'd be fun."

"You will be in restraints, that's for damn sure. And you…" She had turned to the driver, but noticed three shadows appear on the building wall nearby. "Open the doors."

The driver did as he was told, and a moment later Garcia and the other two were peeking out from the side of a building. Valerie beckoned them over, so they ran, stopping at the opened door to look inside.

"Well that worked out," Garcia said. "Got him and one of their pods."

She nodded. "I'm going to have his driver take me to the other two amigos. If he takes me to the wrong spot, this orca dies."

Garcia looked at the CEO, unsure. He looked like he was about to protest, when Sandra moaned and leaned against the pod, head down, and gagged.

Diego was at her side in an instant, one hand on the small of her back, the other holding her hair away from her face.

Noticing Valerie's concerned expression, Garcia said, "It's not the first time," and nodded back to the alley with a hand wave in front of his nose.

Sandra glanced up, biting her lip, and her eyes flitted over to Diego.

"She's going to be okay," Diego said.

"Wait…" Valerie looked between the two, and then her eyes went wide as realization dawned. "You have to be shitting me. Why'd you agree to come on this trip?"

"What?"

"You jackass." Valerie pointed at Sandra. "She's pregnant! Right? I mean, could you be?"

Sandra looked up with wide, scared eyes, but then smiled. "I… I don't know. But I've been wondering ever since leaving Ohio."

"Dammit, Ohio."

"It would've had to have happened before that," Diego

said, blushing. "But after we left, for sure. Had I even the slightest suspicion, there'd be no way we would've come on this mission."

Valerie beamed, looking at her two friends, almost forgetting about the mission at hand until Garcia cleared his throat.

"Huge congrats to everyone involved," the sergeant said. "But here's the thing, we still have this tub o'lard to deal with, and his two compatriots."

"Damn, you're right." Valerie considered the situation, then said, "You three, get him somewhere where his people can't find him, and get his hands tied. I don't want the crazy side of him taking over and orchestrating some sort of escape."

"The FDG taking this guy prisoner?" Garcia's left eye twitched. "That could be trouble."

"Don't worry," Valerie said. "With what I'm about to do? There won't be anyone left to bring trouble."

"Then we have a deal," Garcia said. "But if TH has a problem with it, I'm pointing at you."

"I have no problem with that." She pulled the CEO from the vehicle, took some ties from Garcia and applied restraints, then shoved him over to Garcia. Turning to Sandra, she gave her a hug. "I couldn't be happier for you. Be careful, rest, got it?"

Sandra nodded. "And you… be careful."

"Have I ever had a reason to worry?" Valerie asked.

"Yes. And this time you're going up against two dangerous men, and, from what we understand, a training ground for Forsaken assassins. That doesn't sound like a situation you should be taking lightly."

"Well, when you say it like that. Fine, yes, I'll be careful."

She accepted her sword back, then strapped on her pistol. She turned to Diego. "You got her?"

"Always have, always will." Diego winked, wrapping his arm back around Sandra. "Oh, and keep the pod, we might need it for our trip home."

"The driver's not one of theirs," Garcia said, nodding to the driver. "Or, he wasn't."

"Still isn't," the driver said. "Just doing the job appointed to me."

"Good." Valerie climbed back into the pod, careful with her sword as she did so. "You're with me for now, until this mission's over." She let her eyes flash red. "I find out you left me or did anything to remotely piss me off, we'll have a problem."

The driver nodded.

"Val," Sandra said, with a small wave. "Kick their asses."

"Every last one of them," Valerie said with a laugh that, for a moment, made her wonder if she might have more in common with this CEO guy than she wanted to admit. But no, she thought as the door closed and the pod lifted off. She was just giddy with the thought that, finally, this situation with the CEOs was coming to a close.

CHAPTER TWENTY-ONE

Black Plague HQ

Robin and the others stood at the ready, knowing it was coming, but not sure when. She and Brad had made it back in time to warn Giuseppe, who in turn had warned his superiors. Now they were formed up, ready for war. The plan was to march into Chicago like they had planned, but knowing that a powerful vampire and at least a couple Weres would be up against them meant the CEOs had insisted they be armed to the teeth.

Each vampire had blades lined with silver, special weapons with explosive bullets, the kind that would make vampire healing take longer, and protective gear the CEOs had taken from their elite mercenaries before having them executed for failing to retake Old Manhattan.

A glance back at HQ revealed two silhouettes on top of the walls, looking down. The men they called the CEOs. A third joined them occasionally, and sometimes they would all three take their guards and disappear for days on end. The third, as Robin understood it, was currently in the city working to make bribes and see who he could win over to their side before the attack.

The skinny one raised an arm, and then Giuseppe gave the command to his squad, which included Robin and Brad, leading each of their small teams.

Robin hadn't even taken her first step when a second command came, someone from the front shouting, "Hold!"

They all craned their necks to see what was happening, a low murmur arising from her fellow vampires. Squinting her eyes, Robin saw it—a lone pod approaching. The third CEO, right? So why were they holding? She supposed it could be that he was bringing news, that he had intercepted the vampire and already taken care of her.

Robin certainly hoped that was the case.

But as it drew closer, one of the doors opened, something flashed, and then the sound carried over with a crack. Everyone looked around, confused, until a vampire next to Robin stumbled back. Robin cringed at the sight of blood trickling down his face from a little hole in his forehead.

CRACK! CRACK!

Two more vampires hit, and then they started to realize what was happening.

"Get to cover!" she shouted as she made for HQ with her team on her heels.

"Fall back," Giuseppe shouted, darting past her. "Defensive positions!"

She couldn't believe this. Was Chicago making a move on them? She paused briefly at the gates to the old arena, but looking back all she saw was the singular pod, now spinning to a stop not far off, a lone figure leaping from it to take on several vampires who had charged to meet the danger head-on.

The pod turned back and made its retreat, while the lone figure, a woman, Robin now saw, cut her way through these vampires with ease. She held a large sword in one hand, a pistol in the other, and now ran at a new group of attackers, shooting two before dicing them up.

Robin had never seen anything like it, the way this woman moved with grace and destruction, every stab a precise hit and killing blow. The special gear was doing nothing against this onslaught, the silver blades useless, as they weren't able to hit their mark.

She had to get out of there before it was her at the end of that sword, so she ran in retreat, shoving other vampires aside in her mad dash to find a defensive position within the fortress.

CHAPTER TWENTY-TWO

Black Plague HQ

Valerie was damn glad she'd finished off that vial of blood in the car, but that left her with only one to go. Still, she imagined that getting through this would be fine. It was after that she had to worry about.

For now, she continued the charge.

While she had planned to simply extract the CEOs, she hadn't realized the extent of this assassin training academy, or that they had such grand ambitions. Make a move on Chicago, and eventually even to New York?

Hell to the *no*!

She had to admit, they were good. She smiled

She was better.

A knife flashed before her eyes and she ducked low, following it up with a slice of her sword up and through the vampire, splitting him in half. Another came from behind, so she pushed with her fear to give herself some room and then rolled, removing his feet before coming up for the head.

A command sounded and those nearby collapsed as weapons clicked—BRRRTTT!

Bullets hit the ground nearby, several even connecting with Valerie, and she grunted in pain as she threw herself to the ground and rolled to the other vampires to take cover beneath those she had already felled.

A sniper rifle shot sounded, and her right thigh exploded in pain. Shit, silver! She dug it out and then took another shot to the side, though this one wasn't silver.

She needed to get inside, so pushed with fear again, harder, so that those nearby fell to their knees. They shielded their faces and one screamed as she charged. Heads rolled, blood flowed, and she didn't care one bit that she was shot multiple times. First they would die, then she would allow herself the time to wallow in pain and self-pity.

No, forget that. She'd kill them all then dance on their corpses for what they were planning to do, and for supporting the CEOs and what they had done.

As far as she was concerned, they were all supporting the blood trade against their own kind—in a way, that was like selling out your cousins to be eaten by your neighbors.

If she didn't have time for self-pity because she was going to do a jig in their blood.

Boo-fucking-hoo.

Picking up two bodies at once, she charged forward, barely registering the plethora of bullets ripping the bodies to shreds and the tiny dings as bullets ricocheted off of the armor and hit their own.

Stone rose above and she knew she had reached the gate, so she tossed the bodies at two oncoming vampires, then turned to draw her sword and take down another that had almost caught her from behind.

This time there was no warning their own, but two grenades hit the ground and everyone froze—everyone except Valarie, that is, because she had seen these before. Commander Strake had used similar grenades on her when she had attacked his fortress.

No way in hell was she letting that silver shrapnel hit her again.

With a push of energy, she ran and pushed with a kick off of the nearest vampire, gaining momentum to land on the next vampire over, connecting feet to his chest, and using that to push herself into a backward flip up and over a wall of stunned vampires.

KA-BOOM!

The grenades went off just as Valerie was landing and, although her bullet wounds tore and hurt like crazy, the silver shrapnel was completely absorbed by the wall of vampires. Many of them dropped, shouting in pain, and more screamed and turned in confusion, shooting or hacking at anything nearby.

Valerie almost laughed at the chaotic sight. These jackoffs were doing the work for her.

While she wanted to grab a bag of grapes and sit back to enjoy the show, she had some vampire-hunting big wigs to execute.

No one even seemed to notice as she ducked out of there and ran at vampire speed across the courtyard.

Stairs waited at the far end, seemingly undefended, until the first step sent two walls of silver-lined spikes closing in on her. Her speed was barely enough to escape it, though one of the spikes scraped her heel and tore her shoe.

"Dammit!" she spat out. Good shoes weren't easy to find,

and she certainly didn't want to walk all the way back to Old Manhattan with a torn shoe.

She was about to start cursing a bit more about it, when she noticed she was out of the stairwell, but two doors were closing on each side of her, a green gas blowing in from tubes on either side. Something told her she didn't want to be trapped in here with that gas, no matter how powerful a vampire she was.

Images of herself on a table being drained for blood flashed through her mind, and she ran for the closing door to her left. It was too low to slide under, so she grabbed hold to see if she could lift it.

A jolt of pain through her body told her the door had just electrocuted her.

Seeing no other way out, she gritted her teeth and grabbed hold again, with only several inches of a gap.

The shocks of electricity sent her teeth chattering, but it was only pain, after all. Instead of pulling back this time, she used the pain to fuel her strength, and soon had the door moving the other way. She screamed out in frustration, pulling until the door was at waist level, breathing in that horrible gas that smelled like rotten apples, and then ducked and threw herself forward through the gap.

The door slammed shut behind her, with the gas on the other side. Several stairways before her, Valerie took the one on the left—stick to the left or the right, you'll eventually find your way, while going down the middle, she figured, could lead to endless circles.

The former arena had been converted with much rebuilding. It looked like at times there had been various rooms built here, possibly to house different communities over the years, or possibly used as a prison.

Judging by the old bloodstains on the walls, it had either ended badly or had not been a pleasant place. She went up another flight of stairs and saw something move ahead, then a door closing, so she sprinted and slammed into the door, knocking it off its hinges, and falling inward.

The vampire backpedaled away from her, joining a room of vampires, who all turned to face her. To Valerie's surprise, a young female vampire was on the far side of the room, backing up and cursing. She couldn't have been older than nineteen, in looks anyway.

With vampires, it could be hard to tell.

"You all really want to die today?" Valerie said, smoke rising from her burnt hands and blood dripping from her bullet wounds, even though they were already starting to slowly heal. "I'd really rather save my energy for your bosses, but if this is how it has to be..."

The first charged her, so Valerie, hands stinging with the grip of it, pulled out her sword and ran it through his chest, up into his skull, and then pulled it out so that he was split in two.

"What'd I say?" She pointed the sword to the room. "Can we all just agree that you'll lie down, pretend to be dead, and I'll progress upward?"

A couple of them seemed to be considering this, but then charged. With a sigh, she took a defensive stance and then took these ones down too.

"Listen, you're skilled. I see that." She pulled out her pistol. "But you are all going to be dead by morning at this rate. Any of you that aren't, I'll drag into the sunlight and leave you there to die. Clear?"

To Valerie's disappointment. The rest charged then. But as she commenced with shooting and cutting them down, she noticed the female vampire in the corner, watching with curiosity. Petite, with shortly cropped, light-brown hair, with a bit of a pout to her lips.

Interesting, she thought as she removed another head. She'd have to ask that one what was going through her head before she removed it from the torso.

◈ ◈ ◈

Robin stood in the center of the large room, her fellow vampire assassins charging this demon, this angel of death, and meeting their demise.

Each and every damned one of them.

And as she watched, she realized she felt nothing for these vampires. They fell one after the other, sometimes two at a time, but it failed to move her in the least.

In fact, she wasn't one of them at all. Why should she be helping them? Why should she fight this woman vampire who had come to kill them all? If anything, she should be helping her.

"Ahhh!" Robin shouted as she turned on her own teammates, vampires who she knew had helped capture her, helped sell her family into slavery, and would do so much worse if left alive. She tore through the nearest two, then ran at the next one over, and pulled back just in time to see a long, silver-lined sword cleave his head off.

She stood there in front of the woman, staring, chest heaving, and the two couldn't separate their gaze.

A vampire charged, causing Robin to finally look away. She jabbed both knives into the vampire's chest, but then the woman stepped forward and slashed with the sword, ripping the vampire's head from its body.

"They'll heal from everything else," Valerie said, giving her a nod. "We, I mean."

Robin nodded, hesitating.

"You're on my side?" Valerie asked.

"If you mean to kill these bastards and let me free to find my family, then yes."

"Then great, welcome to team Valerie. That's me by the way. If I had the time, I'd get you a shirt." She nodded, "Check your rear."

Robin spun just in time to see a vampire come at her with his own knives, but she ducked, fast, and came up into his sternum with one of her own. But Valerie had said that the head needs to come off. God, that was sick.

She pushed off, then jammed her second blade into his throat. With her first free now, she stabbed it into the other side of this throat, then pulled on both and twisted, like a crazy pair of scissors, and the vampire's head flew off.

Valerie had been taking care of someone else, but paused to nod her approval. "Keep it up, and you might just get out of here alive."

"I intend to," Robin said, then threw one of the knives to hit a vampire right behind Valerie. He staggered back and fell down the stairs.

She ran past Valerie and yelled, "I'm starting to like that knife."

"Don't let him keep it then!" Valerie called after her, then continued her way up the other set of stairs, with grunts of exertion as she continued to cut down vampire after vampire.

When Robin reached the bottom step and pulled her blade from the vampire's chest, she stared into his dying eyes.

"Giuseppe, you bastard." She laughed, and then sliced into his throat, pushing down until his head rolled aside.

"You'll never force another vampire to drink of the innocent, and you'll damn sure never take another girl from her family, you black-hearted son of a bitch!"

As she stood, a realization hit her—Valerie had just gone up to the upper levels, where Robin and the others had never been allowed. Where the most elite of elite vampires trained and, she imagined, would likely have set up a defensive in case she made it this far.

It was entirely possible Robin was about to lose her ticket out of here.

CHAPTER TWENTY-THREE

Black Plague HQ

Valerie entered the top floor of the arena, what had once been made up of viewing boxes. Old screens lay broken across the ground, couches on their sides and pushed out of the way, so that in the middle awaited a team of six vampires, a seventh in the middle.

This seventh had long, black hair, and was thin, slightly resembling Diego, though she couldn't quite tell his ethnicity. He held a sword in each hand and wore body armor.

"You're the one, I failed to kill," the man said, and then she recognized him.

"In Old Manhattan," she said. "The plan worked then, you thought I was dead?"

"This time, I mean to be certain."

With a flick of his hand, a boy ran forward and presented the man with a helmet that looked like it was made out of similar material as the body armor, though it had a visor of thick, clear material that covered most of his face, so that he was protected but didn't lose much visibility.

He put on the helmet, smiled, and then closed the visor.

This one was clearly better trained than those downstairs, and Valerie had to wonder if the other six fought so well. His swords moved like flashes of light and, without the power Michael had bestowed on her, Valerie was quite certain she would never have survived this attack. Her wounds certainly didn't help, and neither did the fact that the vampire kept aiming for her wounds as he attacked.

At one point in the attack, she had just dodged a feint when she heard a slight whistling sound and felt a prick in the back of her leg.

If they were attacking her from behind, they would have to do a lot better than that. Ignoring all pain, she hacked at the vampire and brought her sword across the vampire's abdomen, then raised it to remove his head.

Only, the strike glanced off his helmet, and her arm fell to her side, heavy.

What was happening?

Another whistle sound and another prick.

Oh, shit. They were pumping her full of some sort of limiting agent. Sure, her body would heal it, push it out, but before they had time to tear her to pieces? She wasn't sure she could bet on it.

She pushed on her fear, but the vampire before her merely staggered back a step before moving back into the advance.

Now she was in full defensive mode, simply throwing her sword to stop his attacks. Her mind was racing for her next move, going between clarity and sluggish annoyance as more darts hit her.

With a gamble, she swung her blade to deflect his, and

then kept the momentum going so that she sliced across one of the other men, just before the next dart would've likely hit her.

A moment of clarity struck, and then she was taking down two more, throwing them at her attacker as she made her way around the room.

Three whistling darts came at her, but she leaped behind a fallen couch, and then thrust her sword upward as her pursuer did the same. It tore into his abdomen, spilling guts, and dropping him to the floor.

He reached out, trying to pull his intestines back inside so he could heal, while she advanced, breathing heavy, pissed.

"That wasn't… very… nice." She focused on her breathing, keeping track of the other vampires in the corners of her eyes, and as soon as one moved, she struck at him and then turned back to the one on the floor, stomped on his helmet repeatedly until it cracked, and then removed his head with her sword.

"AHHH!" one of the others screamed as he ran forward, but then a new round of bullets sprayed across him so that he fell at Valerie's feet.

She quickly removed his head, then looked up to see the vampire girl standing at the top of the stairs.

"You came back."

"Figured you might help me out after this, if I help you now." The girl pursed her lips and then frowned. "Not that I have any reason to trust you, aside from what my gut's telling me."

"It's a good thing to trust," Valerie said, turning to eye the dead man and his nasty guts. "You know, as long as it's all in one piece."

"Let's see that it stays that way then. The name's Robin."

"Valerie," Valerie nodded to the attacker moving Robin's way. "You want me to…?"

"If you don't mind."

"Not at all."

Valerie picked up a semi-automatic from the ground and pumped the vampire full of rounds. As he fell to his knees, she walked up, adjusted her stance so the blood would fly away from Robin, and then hacked at the guy's throat. It took three hacks because of the armor, but when the head fell off, she looked back up at Robin with a smile.

A pounding of feet on stairs behind them pulled their attention, and a moment later a young male vampire came into view.

Valerie aimed in on him, but Robin shouted, "Wait!" and lunged, knocking the rifle aside.

In an instant, Valerie had a sword to her throat, eyes darting between the newcomer and her. "Explain!"

"Not him, please," Robin said, then took a step back, hands raised in submission. "Just not him… he—he's like a brother to me."

"A brother?" the newcomer said, holding his blades at the ready. He turned to Valerie with confusion, then looked around at the mess of bodies. "What is this?"

"Brad, just, please…" Robin stepped toward him, motioning for him to lower the blades. "Put down your weapons."

He frowned, staring at her in confusion. "You'd throw away everything? All of this?"

"None of this is me. I never wanted to be a vampire, I never asked to be torn away from my family and told I had to kill to survive!"

He bit his lip, clearly torn apart, more footsteps pounded behind him, and shouting.

Valerie lowered her sword and nodded at him. "Your move. I intend to kill the men up there, and anyone standing in my way. You can help this girl, this sister," she noticed him wince and realized that he saw their relationship in a different light, so added, "this woman, who I see you care very much about. Dying at my hand won't help you in any possible way."

With a clearing of his throat, he nodded to Robin and said, "Just know… I'd do anything for you."

He turned, weapons at the ready, and shouted a war cry as he retreated to take on the approaching vampires, buying Valerie and Robin more time.

"I—I want out of here," Robin said, looking like she was going to be sick. "They forced me, took me from my family."

If this was true, Valerie had no choice but to free this girl and avenge her. Luckily, the avenging part was already in progress.

"You going to help him?" Valerie asked.

"He can fend for himself."

"Then stay close," Valerie motioned to the girl and together they advanced to a ladder that led up to the roof. The final showdown.

◈ ◈ ◈

Robin followed Valerie, though careful to keep just enough distance. She had no idea if this vampire lady was what the others had told her, or what her gut was saying right now. More than anything, she wanted to believe that she was what she appeared to be—someone hell-bent on destroying these CEOs and the system of vampires they had created.

Seeing as this system had been exactly what took her

family and made her a vampire, she was one-hundred percent on board.

They emerged onto the roof, gusts of wind blowing at them so that Valerie's clothes flapped around her, making cracking noises. Robin's body armor was stable, naturally, but she could feel the chill of the wind through its cracks and it made her shiver.

That, or maybe it was the sight of this powerful being, this woman who had been the grief of these powerful CEOs, the reason they had created their army of vampire assassins.

And now she was their destruction.

Two forms appeared before them, at the far side of the roof. As they approached, they could see by the moonlight creeping out from behind thick, gray clouds, the forms of a large, muscular man, and a petite woman.

"You've found us," the woman said, stepping forward.

Robin hadn't been so close to them before, and in truth had never considered that the one they called Alex might be a woman. That must mean the tall one was Dmitri.

"If you are the other two members of the trio referred to in Old Manhattan as the CEOs," Valerie stepped forward, sword held out at her side, "or the Three Amigos by those who would mock you, then I'd advise you say your prayers and prepare to meet your maker."

"Stupid girl," Dmitri said in a heavy, almost Russian accent. "We are the makers. Everything that exists is because we allow it to."

"Including you, you pitiful excuse for a blood bag," Alex said, stepping forward and pulling two arch rods from her waist. She flipped them on and blue sparks burst forth, crossing from one to the other.

"You two never should have hunted my kind," Valerie

said. She motioned to Robin, who almost wished she could just turn around and avoid all this, but knew she could never escape while these two were still alive. "And what you have done to these people? It's sick. For that, it's time you face your judgment."

Valerie moved her shoulders, trying to get a kink out, "Justice rules here, not you two."

Dmitri smiled and cracked his neck, then his knuckles, stepping up to Alex's side. He pulled out a weird looking gun, one like Robin had never seen before. And aimed. "Let's see how you two like being drained for the rest of your pitiful lives."

Robin pulled her blades and, as Valerie moved left, she moved right.

The woman came her way, arc rods lighting up the night, and Robin noted the shots coming from Dmitri's gun, like balls of electricity that sparked red. One caught Valerie in the leg and sent her flying back, then another caught her in the chest and sent her into a series of electrocution-induced convulsions.

Robin dodged an arc rod, using her vampire speed to move around the woman, but a wall of electricity went up between the two, then shot out at her and knocked her back to the edge of the roof.

Well damn, this wasn't going to be easy.

◈ ◈ ◈

Valerie's brain felt like mush as the electric waves coursed through her and seemed to eat her from the inside out. She caught brief glimpses of the young vampire, Robin, getting thrown back, trying to attack again, and a wave of electricity throwing her back again.

These bastards weren't playing fair. They weren't accepting their judgment lying down, which meant Valerie would have to teach them how.

Another red shot came her way, but this time she fought the pain and rolled aside, then hit the rooftop door. She rolled back, pulling it in front of her as another shot came, and then tore it from its hinges and heaved it at the man.

The door slammed into him and his gun went flying across the roof. The wind blew heavy and she had to steady herself, then charged forward to snatch up her sword and move in for the woman. Almost there, the door came back at her, hitting her in the shoulder and knocking her over.

How could he have recovered so fast? With the wind whipping around them, she couldn't smell which direction the attacks were coming from or sense their movements. All her mind-reading could pick up was fiery hatred, and when she pushed fear, Dmitri just laughed.

"We've surrounded ourselves with vampires and Weres our whole lives," he said, ignoring his discarded gun and pulling out a long blade, much like her own, though this one was serrated on one side and half as long, with a metal hand guard. "You think we don't know terror?" he snickered, "We feed on terror!"

Robin grunted behind her, and Valerie glanced back to see the younger vampire had finally gotten past Alex's defense and scored a cut across the woman's breast, but the cost was an arc rod jammed into her gut, another on her chest, for a combined thrust that sent her spinning through the air.

Not waiting for Dmitri to make his move, Valerie turned on Alex, but the woman anticipated it and came around with a sweeping arc of electricity that, after the pain Valerie had felt on the ground moments before, caused her to hesitate. She cursed herself as she realized what had happened—these two were a team and were playing off of each other.

It was confirmed when she realized she had hesitated just long enough for Dmitri to reach her with a strike that brought his sword down across her shoulder. Valerie was quick enough to move with the strike so that it only tore a chunk of flesh away with the blade's serrated edge.

It hurt like hell, but gave her the momentum she needed to roll aside, landing right next to Robin.

The younger woman's eyes showed defeat, all hope seemingly gone.

"We have to work as a team," Valerie said. "I don't know how they're moving so fast, but they are working together. I'm beaten to hell, and so are you, so they have that advantage. But together, we can take them."

Robin glanced over, a flash of hope in her eyes, and then pulled herself up to one knee. Valerie hopped up and took her hand, helping her to stand. Together they faced their attackers, and, as fast as she could, Valerie drank half the last vial of blood, then handed it to Robin. Oddly, the young vampire winced at the sight of it.

"Drink," Valerie hissed. "Then come behind me so they don't see you, and at the last minute, you move left at the same moment I do. Keep it so we have two on one."

As their attackers moved in, Valerie darted forward to meet them. Playtime was over. She felt Robin behind her, and then caught a whiff of something she hadn't expected—Were?

It was too late to think about it, she had to make her move. The team of Dmitri and Alex were strong, but one at a time, they were nowhere near as powerful as Valerie, and definitely not as powerful as Valerie and Robin combined. Though she barely knew this girl, already she was impressed.

She was about to put her to the test.

"Now!" she shouted, and darted left as she swept out with her sword at Dmitri's feet—but it was just a fake, as her real strike came a second later when she diverted the sword's path, lifted, and thrust back down into the back of his calf.

He howled in pain, and then Robin was there on the other side of him, silver blades tearing into him.

Alex shouted in frustration at seeing what they had done, and tried to work her way around to flank them. But Valerie used Dmitri's moment of weakness to roll over him and land a kick square in the woman's chest.

The blow threw her back, concaving her chest so that, when she tried to move again, she gasped for breath and blood flew from her mouth. When she tried to thrust the one arc rod remaining forward, Valerie knocked it aside with ease and then caught her with a side kick that threw her into the side the roof, which she hit and then toppled over, screaming until they heard a crunch far below.

"NO!" Dmitri shouted, snatching up one of the arc rods and turning it on Robin, who was still using him as a pin cushion. It threw her back, and then he turned on Valerie and charged in spite of his limp and the blood pouring from his leg.

She was ready and had been expecting an attack. She caught him square in the stomach with her sword, so that it came out of his back, but he had his massive arms around her, and together they went flying over the side of the roof, following in Alex's wake.

In the poor condition Valerie was in, this was going to suck terribly, she thought.

She released the sword and slammed her head into Dmitri's so that his nose broke and blood went flying, but more importantly, he loosened his grasp enough for her to break free. With a yell of frustration and exertion, she used his body's momentum to maneuver him underneath her, so that when they slammed into the ground moments later, she landed with her knees on his chest and then went rolling across the ground.

It still hurt like hell, but she was able to push herself up. Each breath was a pain, and she imagined something had broken in her chest—a rib puncturing a lung, perhaps?

Pushing herself up, she turned to Dmitri and stared. He was pushing himself up too, and then she caught on—the whiff of Were from above. Of course.

Others were fighting still, and then she recognized the young man Robin had stood up for, and a moment later, Robin at his side, and soon all had stopped to watch as Dmitri found his footing. He was shouting, furious, as he pulled the sword from himself and tossed it aside.

Almost instantly, the wound began to heal, and all around them, gasps came from vampires. They had apparently not realized he was a Were. Never been close enough to catch his scent, she imagined.

With a roar, Dmitri tore his clothes from his body as he transformed into the largest wolf Valerie had ever seen. He was even larger than those from the Golden City, and almost the size of a bear on its four legs.

"Fuck me," she said, every inch of her body screaming out in pain, then braced herself as it charged.

She knelt down, one hand on the ground, knees bent, and her eyes glowed red with such brilliance that she could see the rubble before her glowing. Her fangs emerged and her vampire blood pumped with the adrenaline of the fight.

There was no way she was going to sit there and wait for him, so she pushed off, growling, prepared to meet the beast. It leaped and she drew her claws and then slid underneath it, reaching up to tear into its belly. She pushed herself up and leaped for her sword where it had fallen, still covered in his blood, then rolled to pick it up and turn.

A cheer sounded and at first she thought it was for her, but when she turned, she realized that many more here were still rooting for that bastard. He had recovered from her attack, blood dripping from multiple areas across his body, but he wasn't giving up. He charged again, and this time went for her legs, mouth open wide.

She scoffed, lifting the sword to remove his head, but saw too late that he had come at her with a fake attack. At the last minute, he pushed off and transformed, landing so that he trapped her sword arm against her body, legs wrapped around her, and began landing elbow after elbow against her face.

It almost hurt enough to make her get over the fact that he was pressed up against her, naked. Almost.

Yuck, she thought as she bit the next elbow that came—it slammed into her mouth and hurt like hell, but when he pulled back she tore into him and flesh separated into a bloody mess.

He howled and transformed back, teeth sinking into her neck and she actually screamed, to her surprise. If his jaws were as strong as she suspected they were, he might actually be able to separate her head from her body, and that would be the end for her.

From the corner of her eye, she saw Robin move forward, but held up a hand. This was her fight.

The wolf must've counted on it ending fast, because he was now exposed to her sword, if she could get the angle.

Risking the pain, she fell to her side and brought the sword behind the wolf, pulling it with her free hand so that it cut into the back of its neck.

More growls came, but mixed with a terrified whimper.

It was down to this Were's jaw power versus her vampire strength and the sharpness of her sword.

Unfortunately for him, she had been provided the strength she needed to get the job done. With a final shout of frustration, she pulled and felt the sword grind through bone.

A moment later, the wolf's teeth released her neck and she was gasping for breath. The head rolled aside, the body going limp.

Not a single muscle wanted to respond, but she forced herself to stand, to look strong, even though she knew she probably looked like she was already dead. Blood gushed down her shoulder, and elsewhere, but with the adrenaline and recent drink of blood, she could already feel it starting to heal. A warmth filled her as she focused on the healing, and she could almost imagine pulling on a power from beyond, like another dimension even, and felt the wounds heal even faster.

As the blood flow stopped, she looked around at the gathered vampires, and finally rested her gaze on Robin.

"It's over."

Robin stepped forward and nodded. "Do you mind?"

Valerie shook her head, not sure what Robin had in mind, but figuring she'd give her the benefit of the doubt.

She turned back to face the others. "Many of you were taken against your will, forced into this lifestyle. Some of you embraced it, perhaps all… I don't think we need to ask questions, except for one." With a look of wanting confirmation Valerie's way, waiting for the nod Valerie gave her, she said, "Where do you go from here? Are you going to be the vampire these people wanted you to be, or are you going to say forget that bullshit, and work to make the world a better place?"

Several stepped forward, nodding, but others remained hesitant, casting frightened glances Valerie's way.

Perhaps Robin had a point. Having more warriors was never a bad thing, but could she trust them? Not likely, but she could at least work on finding out which ones she could trust, and that started with tonight.

"You might have heard of me," Valerie said, stepping up to Robin's side. "This woman, she had never *met* me, but gave me her trust. She did so because she wanted a better life. Vampires don't have to be bad, there is no reason that you should be. We can live right alongside everyone else, even the Weres. If you are trustworthy and loyal, you can join us. Come back to Old Manhattan, join the defensive forces of that city, and you will not only become a part of a community, but a family."

The rest looked among themselves, and then more stepped forward, while others, only a handful remaining, turned and fled.

"Should we go after them?" Robin said.

Valerie hesitated. "I've never preached killing for killing's sake, but running means they have declared themselves the enemy. Am I wrong?"

Robin shook her head, no.

"Then yes, let it be a test. The rest of you all, stop them so that this pattern of evil no longer continues. Carry out my justice… because now's as good a time as any."

The assassin vampires nodded, and then ran off, all but Robin.

"Do your really mean to take them back with you?"

Valerie cocked her head. "Them?"

"I have somewhere else to go."

"I see." Valerie walked over and leaned against the wall, pleased to see the pod approaching in the distance. Apparently, the driver had figured out it was over. "Here's the thing, Robin, I don't know if I'm going back either."

"But you said…?"

"Oh yes, they will be able to go to the city, as long as they pass some tests my people will have for them. They'll be kept on external defensive positions until their trust is earned, but they'll be accepted."

"And you?"

"My return would be awkward."

"You being dead and all?" Robin asked with a smirk.

Valerie laughed. "That would be it. Well, that and the fact that I don't know… it's been over a month since I left. I thought more than anything that I'd miss a certain someone there, but, I don't know. Yes, I miss him, but more in a friendly I-wonder-what-he's-doing kind of way. If I go back, what life's there for me? Hiding in the shadows? Will he expect romance, or do I hide from him too?"

Robin shook her head, "This is all way over my head."

"Yes, I guess it would be." Valerie laughed again. "I don't suppose everyone you meet opens up like this?"

"You *did* just go through a lot, it makes sense."

Valerie nodded, thinking back to everything she had gone through. Everything she had set out to do, at least on a high level, was basically accomplished. America was still in disarray, sure, and she would certainly do her part to see that groups like this and the CEOs didn't rise up again. But the immediate problems she had been presented with all seemed to have been resolved.

She leaned her head back, closing her eyes. "It's actually over. I mean, I set out to do so much and, in a way, it's over." She opened her eyes again at the sound of the pod door opening. Robin was staring at her. "What about you? What's your plan from here?"

"I told you about my family. Well, I'm going to find them."

"Couldn't they be anywhere by now, if they're…?"

"Still alive?" Robin bit her lip, but then said, "I've thought of that, but I have to know. I've heard rumors, about slavery up north. The warmer climate and all… Something to do with that, anyway."

"North?" A trigger went off in Valerie's head. "I don't suppose any of those rumors had to do with pirates?"

"Actually, yes."

"We might just be headed in the same direction then," Valerie said with a smile. "I mean, I have to see my friends home, we just found out one of them is pregnant, after all."

"Congratulations, I mean, maybe? In this world, is that a good thing?"

Valerie nodded. "If we want to bring joy into this world, change it for the better, then yes. I can't think of anything more joyful."

For a long moment, Valerie looked out at the surrounding vampires, a little less than two-dozen, it appeared, and nodded.

"Who are you?" she asked. "I don't mean, like what's your name, but… who are you really? Do you remember?"

"I do, but I'm scared I'll forget. Parts are already hazy.

The faces of my parents, for instance. I can see them laughing, and I have this image in my head that I'm certain will never go away, of my mother sobbing, my father holding her and stroking her hair. I remember that, even though I just reached adulthood, they were already searching for a spouse for me. Trying to marry me off. Not to get rid of me, but because they thought a man could protect me in this crazy world." She scoffed. "Imagine that, considering what I've become. But even back then, I'm pretty sure I could've taken most men in this world. A couple tried, wanted their way with me without my permission… ask them whether I can hold my own or not."

Valerie laughed. "I'll take your word for it."

"Who am I, though?" Robin continued. "I'm their daughter, and I'll stop at nothing until I find them."

Valerie's smile vanished as she said, "Hold onto those memories, Robin. They fade fast, and that's when you start losing yourself."

For a long while, they stood there in silence, with Valerie struggling to find anything from her past. An image of herself playing by a river, then walking among tall reeds, staying low and hiding, her feet soaked, as a band of raiders passed.

Life had been tough, and always would be. But if she could find a way to make it less so, she damn sure would.

"It's settled then," she said to Robin. "You lead them, following the pod, back to Old Manhattan. Then you and I will head north, where you'll embark on a journey to find your family, and I'll bring justice to a bunch of slave-taking, shipment-stealing pirates."

"That sounds pretty damn good to me," Robin said with a nod of her head.

"What about…?" Valerie glanced over to Brad, who was

holding a pow-wow with some of the vampires.

"Keep him in New York. He can keep the vampires in line."

"All that stuff about him being like a brother to you?"

"Totally true," Robin said, averting Valerie's gaze and blushing, "but he seems to want so much more than that, and… it's not exactly the way I work."

Valerie tilted her head, considering what that meant, then smiled knowingly. "Have it your way. It'll be easier for us to get around with fewer people."

Robin smiled with a nod, and a look that roamed across Valerie's body that made her wonder if the younger vampire was assessing the wounds, or checking her out in an entirely different way.

This trip was going to be interesting.

CHAPTER TWENTY-ONE

Old Manhattan, Enforcer HQ

Jackson glared at Colonel Donnoly and Sergeant Wallace, then leaned in and said, "Could you repeat that?"

"They're gone," Wallace said. "Cammie and Royland. A Were and a vampire came to me this morning and told me they had been appointed by the two to take their place, and that they were off, but that they had every intention of someday returning."

"Well that's great," Jackson threw his hands up. "Someday? Real fucking specific."

"The point of us calling you here wasn't so you could throw a tantrum," Donnoly said, earning a smile from Wallace. "We need to know that you're on our side, to see what you've heard on the streets."

Jackson leaned back, focusing on controlling his breathing. "Truth is, if they were going to leave, now's the perfect time to do it."

"Your report is similar to ours, I take it?"

"If by that you mean that we seem to have cracked down on all the bars that anyone might have hinted at as being involved in the blood trade. After the unfortunate event with Morgan," he paused to see if they responded to the name in any way, interested to see the knowing look in Wallace's gaze, but a blank stare from Donnoly, "infighting and internal terrorism has been non-existent. There's still the issue of piracy of our goods, but that's external, and something I'm sure we will be dealing with later."

"I'm sure we will," Donnoly said with a pleased nod.

"And… no word on Valerie?"

Wallace shook his head. "It's been too long. I think it's best to assume she isn't coming back. Don't wait for her."

"Harsh," Jackson said, but tilted an imaginary cowboy hat as he said, "Thank you for the kind words, pardner."

He stood and headed for the door, but was intercepted moments later by Wallace.

"He'll never find out," Wallace whispered.

"What?"

"About the warehouse. We know you were involved. Well, at least I do. Point is, stay low, and please, try not to take the law into your own hands. We have the police force for a reason."

Jackson just smiled, nodded, and headed for the door.

"Mr. Mercer," Wallace called after him. "Remember, you're not Valerie. Just because you *were* her boyfriend, doesn't mean you will be able to go on unchecked. I hope I've made myself clear."

Jackson paused at the elevator, pressed the button, and turned around. The idea of saying "Yes" or "Crystal" made him want to shoot himself at that moment, so instead he just imagined himself giving Wallace the middle finger, while actually he smiled, nodded, and then said 'fuck it' and took the stairs.

With Royland and Cammie gone, he knew a lot of the underground protection of the city would fall to him and his people. Wallace had best just stay out of his way.

◈ ◈ ◈

Outside Old Manhattan

The month-long journey back had been rather uneventful, aside from Sandra's nausea and Diego's over-protectiveness. Regular nomad groups must have known not to mess with such a large force with a pod at their lead, while members of the UnknownWorld would have sensed there were a large number of vampires and one Were among the group.

It had been nice to meet TH and the others of Chicago. Before heading out, he had treated them to a steak dinner, a benefit of a recent farm they had started. She had to admit, fresh steak was a thousand times better than the imported meat they had in Old Manhattan. After eating, TH had taken her aside, given her a firm handshake, and told her he had heard all about the plans of the Black Plague, and what she had done for Chicago.

"You ever need my help, you let me know," he had said. "In fact…"

"Yes?"

"If you're interested, depending on how it's going in New York and all, I don't mean to overstep my place, but I think it would be fine if you came with us."

"I'm not sure I'm following, Colonel."

TH smiled and said, “We have plans… big plans. The type that involve a journey that way.” He pointed to the sky, and smiled. “Ever dreamed of going into space, Valerie?”

Honestly, she never had. The idea made her dizzy, and she told him that would be a very big life choice, one she would have to think about. He told her that she had time, and gave her some more specifications before saying farewell. Then he mentioned one name, a name that made her more interested than ever: Bethany Anne.

She had such a curiosity around the legendary vampire, the woman Michael would, as she understood it, be reconnecting with once Akio and Yuko found him. She promised TH to try and return, if everything else worked out.

Then they had set out, the group of vampires with their tents and protective clothing. They rested under shelter during the day as much as possible, wearing their protective clothing otherwise.

This worked fine for Sandra, as Valerie had insisted she only walked when riding in the pod was becoming too much and she wanted to stretch her legs. As if taking her on this journey while pregnant wasn’t enough guilt.

On their way back, they stopped in Cleveland, Ohio, and paid their respects to Gerald. He welcomed the news of what had happened with the Black Plague, and agreed that he and his people would start expanding, looking for others who they could take into his flock, to prepare for an America that would rise from the ashes.

That night, Valerie had found Robin at the edge of the nearby lake, staring out across the water.

“They’re somewhere out there,” the young vampire said. “Possibly looking back toward me right now.”

"We're going to find them." Valerie wrapped an arm around her and squeezed.

"We?"

Valerie shrugged. "You. Me. We. I mean, if I'm going that way to deal with the pirates anyway, I figure it makes sense to stick with you, at least at first."

Robin looked up at her, hopefulness mixed with uncertainty, and nodded. "Thank you."

They waited a day, resting and enjoying casual conversations with the members of Gerald's flock, and the next night were back on the road. The more time Valerie spent with Sandra and Diego, the more time she realized how hard it was going to be to say goodbye. Because of that, she ended up walking and talking with Robin more and more. At least she knew the journey north wouldn't be with someone she couldn't stand.

They finally reached the outskirts of Old Manhattan, where a scout had noticed them coming and sent for Wallace. He arrived to meet them, waiting under the sky that was still purple and blue in the pre-dawn.

Valerie was holding Sandra, who seemed to be fighting back the tears.

"You're going to be an amazing mom," Valerie said.

"Don't say it like that." Sandra pulled back, glaring. "You say it like you'll never come back to find out."

"I'll try, but who knows how long this pirate shit will take, right?"

Sandra nodded. "No, I get it, I just don't want you to verbalize it. Makes it seem more real."

"Deal. Avoid reality when around Sandra. Check."

"Shut up," Sandra said, then gave her a light punch in the arm. "Stay safe out there."

Valerie scoffed. "The word safe should never be used when addressing me."

"Too true," Diego said, reminding the women he was there. The rest had all gone on ahead, all but Robin, who waited at Valerie's side.

Other than that, Wallace was the only one they had told about this new addition to the forces. Valerie reminded him to be extra diligent, and ensure their trustworthiness before giving them any independent roles.

Valerie gave Sandra another hug, and then it was Diego's turn, but he just smiled and said, "We're gonna miss you, Val."

"And I'll miss you two, most of all."

Wallace stepped up next, and asked, "North, huh?"

She nodded.

"I'm not sure how you would've heard, but… Cammie and Royland just went that way themselves. Only left a few days back, you might even catch them."

"I leave them in charge of the city, and they take off on a… what? Don't tell me they're a couple now and this is like some honeymoon thing."

He laughed. "No, though rumor is they've been more friendly lately, in that trying not to let others see way, and failing miserably at that. Another shipment issue, so I think they figured it was best to try and cut the issue off at the knees. And besides, don't worry. We've got this, and they left backfills in place."

"Backfills," Valerie snorted. "Have we become so corporate?"

Wallace laughed at that. "Honestly, we kind of have. Corporatizing the peace. But this time, let's leave any talk of CEOs out of it." He looked at her a moment longer, then said, "You don't want to say goodbye to anyone … er … else?"

She shook her head. "The rest will get it, and Jackson... it would be weird, you know?"

He shook his head. "Not exactly. When it comes to relationships, lately, I feel like I'm a wave that just keeps crashing against the rocks. It fucking hurts."

"You'll make it happen," she assured him. "Just, maybe avoid the Enforcers next time, you know?"

"Trust me, I do."

They shook hands and she pulled him in for a hug.

"Thank you for everything," she said. "And please, protect this city. It means a lot to me."

"I will," he said, and then with a nod to Robin and the others—all in their protective gear to ward off the sun—turned to follow the rest of them into the city.

Without another word, because she wanted to be left to her thoughts for the time being, Valerie turned north and started walking. She knew Robin wasn't far behind, because occasionally the wind would bring her sweet scent, vampire mixed with molasses. An odd one for sure, but pleasant.

It wasn't long before they reached a small hill where Valerie stopped to look back at the city. It was crumbling apart at the edges, with buildings that had never been rebuilt after the great collapse forming a circle around the pristine buildings such as Enforcer HQ.

"You sure you're ready for this?" Valerie asked when Robin joined her and stood at her side.

Robin glanced over, a sparkle of excitement in her eyes mostly hidden by the protective goggles, and said, "You could say I was born ready, if you count vampire life as being reborn. Reborn ready, I guess."

Valerie smiled, wrapped an arm around her new friend, and watched the sunrise come up over the city again. Robin rested her head on Valerie's shoulder, and together they watched the city go from purple to red to yellow, and then the rays of sunlight shoot past the buildings in an almost angelic symbol of the good fortune their journey would bring. Valerie brought her hand up as the rays of light hit them, so as to protect Robin, and then they turned to find some shelter and rest.

They had no idea what this adventure was going to look like, and had a long way to go. For now, they simply enjoyed the moment.

Kicking ass could be left for another day.

AUTHOR'S NOTES - JUSTIN SLOAN

Written: April 2, 2017

The fourth book in a series is always a challenge, especially when it's the end of one arc and the setup for the next. Are all the loose ends closed, or closed enough that readers will feel content to take a breather until they are opened up again in the next set of books? Do readers know what's coming next, and is it engaging enough to make them want to go out and buy book five when it finally comes out?

I certainly hope I have achieved this, and would love to hear from you all about it. JustinSloanAuthor@gmail.com for this or any other author communications.

But let's back up a step and fill you in on where I was when finishing this book. For years now I've been writing on the side, whenever I could, and this was especially challenging for the last four, or since my daughter was born, and then two years later with my son. It has been A LOT of sleepless nights. I mean a lot. To get my writing done, I would take lunch breaks to write, stay up until midnight, and sometimes wake up at 4:00 am to write some more.

But all this is changing… kind of. Because of you AMAZING readers and Michael Anderle, I am focusing on these collaborations and have decided to give the author thing a go—I quit my job and am going to be a full-time author!

I hope this means that, since I'm writing all day, I can get more sleep at night. My editors know what I mean when I say that my writing will improve. So much of my writing the first three books in this series happened while I was nodding off to sleep. I would drink coffee, write a couple of paragraphs, and then realize I had fallen asleep, because a bunch of SSSSSSssss…. JUST JOKING! But like that, I would see those lines of letters or whatever, and realize I had fallen asleep. This happened A LOT.

So can you imagine what it will be like going from that to actually getting sleep and having full days to write? It will be a DREAM COME TRUE.

I'm ecstatic. My wife is ecstatic. I hope you all are too. You made this dream come to life as much as I did, so I hope you can join me in feeling like you accomplished something great. You changed my life! All of you!

Now, if you're the person who reads this and then goes out and gives me a bad review… I still got nothing but love for you, because those negative reviews help narrow down these books to who my proper audience is. I still prefer the positive ones, and will take a moment to ask that if you did enjoy this book, to please go leave a review. And same with the others. And ask that if you enjoy my writing, to please give my other books a chance too.

Here's why: I did an experiment between books three and four in the Reclaiming Honor series. I took the time to write my sequel to *Hounds of God*, titled *Hounds of Light*. It's a werewolf, vampire, and magic story, and I figured that, since I'm having success here, those should do well too.

I was pretty damn wrong. The first book in that series did well, published back in December (it has 79 reviews now!), but book 2 basically flopped.

Shucks.

So the good news there is that I'm committed to writing lots of books with Michael Anderle, at least as long as he will let me. But guess what? I would have done that regardless! I love writing in this world, and I love you all as fans in this world. So really it didn't change anything, except for the fact that, now that I'll be full-time, I would like to do about one or two Kurtherian Gambit books a month, and one of my own every other month.

If my own books don't sell so well, is there a point to do this? My thought is yes, because more books mean more chances to build up more of an audience. Maybe that will mean more readers coming into the Kurtherian Gambit universe who have never read any of these books? That would be awesome! Or maybe it just means that, someday, if Michael runs out of stuff for me to write, I can stand on my own.

It would be great to know that this full-time author situation will last.

So yeah, any help with reading, spreading the word, or even just emailing me to let me know your opinions on the matter would be SUPER helpful and appreciated.

And that takes me on to my next thing I wanted to share: Isn't the new Age of Magic series awesome? In fact, I love the concept so much… I'm going to write an Age of Magic series with Michael! You heard it here first. I will definitely be writing more Valerie books, and yes, Robin is going to be a big part of those, I think, but because I'm going full-time I will have time to do a bit of both. I hope you give the current ones a chance, and I hope you give mine a chance when they come out. They are going to be so fun! I'm all giddy looking at the cover art that has been coming in, and have a guy working on a map already.

I'll stop now, but only after you let me say one more time how amazing life is, and Michael, for allowing me this opportunity. I have LOVED getting to know you all over the last few months, and can't wait to share more adventures and Facebook messages with you all. Your reviews inspire me, and your personal messages remind me why we do this.

Thank you.

On to the next book!

With love,
Justin

AUTHOR'S NOTES - MICHAEL ANDERLE

Written: April 4, 2017

My turn!

THANK YOU for reading another one of our books in The Kurtherian Gambit Universe. It is a pleasure to have the opportunity to tell our stories and have the fans react.

(Lots more fun since the reactions are positive!)

When we set off on this little adventure with Valerie, it was an interesting experiment on collaboration and wondering 'what if.'

What if I could help another author by collaboration? Could I help them enough to help them attain readers? Would fans like a story with other authors writing in the Kurtherian Universe?

Would they (you fans) yell at me because I was screwing up the timeline?

The answer is yes.

Yes, you fans DO like other stories, and yes, you DO yell at me for screwing up the timelines!

There isn't much I can do at the moment about the timelines because the authors that are working with me are authoring freaks of nature ™ (smile). What I mean by that, is so many of them make my relatively rapid pace of production seem anemic. I wanted to write in other areas, and we just decided to 'go for it.'

I felt like this time, I had replaced my Indie Publishing (Author) Outlaw hat with an Indie Publishing (Publisher)

Outlaw hat, and we all just said, "Fuck it! Our fans will go on this crazy messed-up ride with us… *we hope*!"

And you have. Otherwise, you wouldn't be reading this author note, and you won't know that I said this. So, for EVERY one of you reading this, I'm *100%* accurate.

Well, damn. So long as you are reading this in the back of the book – and someone didn't just clip out all of the Author Notes as you are reading those as a set…

Sumbitch. Ok, I'm *MOST LIKELY* right! Hahahahaha.

I digress. So, I'm really digging the authors getting together to make sure they aren't stepping on each others writing toes. Justin and Craig Martelle (the Author of Terry Henry Walton Chronicles series – where the FDG comes from) worked to make sure those parts of the story were right in voice, character and concepts, even though Craig won't be up to this timeline I think until maybe books 8 or 9 perhaps. That is the hallmark (to me) of some fabulous people.

Justin mentioned the Age of Magic, and I guess I can admit we have another Age that will be opening in a few short weeks. This time, it is in outer space where Bethany Anne and the Etheric Empire kicked ass and took names. It is AFTER Bethany Anne, and her core team left the area, but the Etheric Empire and Lance Reynolds (among a few others) stick around.

Lance tells Bethany Anne, "I ain't up to running around the damned universe. Just come see me every five years or so, and we can catch up."

For those wondering what will happen after TKG21?

There's your hint.

Love, Cokes, and Tacos,

Michael

p.s. We are about one and a half hours from releasing this book to the fans, may you all enjoy it, and may you read it like crazy.

SHORT STORY

From Justin: I included this short story as a special treat, because why not. It's a bit of a prequel to a Space Marine novel series I'm doing with a couple of guys, and I figured this is a fun way to share that, but make it special in that we won't include what you see below in those books, and it won't be available on Amazon. I hope you enjoy!

◈ ◈ ◈

Mackie stared at the wall and the contours of paint that formed lines like the clouds, wishing he could think of such mundane things forever, instead of this damned alien invasion.

The Syndicate, everyone was calling them. Supposedly a message had made its way in through Central Command, demanding all militaries across the world lay down arms and submit, or face utter annihilation.

Some here in the U.S. had run to join the Marines, the first to fight, because they promised citizenship, a better life, and if you were desperate enough, a way to escape the lives of mediocrity or, in most cases, poverty.

But not Mackie. No way in hell would he join that slaughter machine, not after what they had done in Latin America, and elsewhere before. Those fucking Marines and their actions had been all over the news. Some claimed they had gone rogue, others said it was all black ops.

Mackie knew the truth, because he knew people in the Resistance, people who shared what they heard with him.

The order had come from the UN itself, to be carried out by the world's strongest fighting force. Go in, don't worry about casualties, and remove the heads of three different Resistance factions in one swift move. Sure, it had set the Resistance back dearly, but whoever had issued the command had clearly not considered how many men and women would be that much more willing to join the Resistance after such actions.

He had tried to convince his neighbor, Quinn, that there were other ways out of her condition, and that joining the Marines was one of the worst possible options. That the Resistance could provide the protection she so longed for, not for herself, but for her little girl, Sammy.

Instead, Quinn had enlisted the day after the invasion message came over the channels. Now it was on every news station—the countdown timer. He could hear it through the walls, and it was almost time.

Like fucking New Years Eve, he thought. Except, instead of a ball dropping here, it would be the end of the world as they knew it.

He stared at the wall, counting with it, "Five, four, three…" He closed his eyes, unable to continue, and then he heard the voice carrying through the wall, little Sammy, only nine years old.

"Zero," she said, and he mouthed it along with her.

The room darkened, and Mackie turned to the sliding glass doors that led out to his apartment balcony. Already the sky was full of invading ships—long and narrow, almost mistakable as Air Force jets, but not quite.

Something was shooting out of them, coming straight for the city. A bunch of somethings, actually. Metallic objects with wings, like gliders, somewhat, and what looked like individuals diving to the earth in red, metallic suits, shooting fire boosters from their feet when they were close, to slow their descent.

The invasion had begun. A crash sounded and the

building shook, and then Sammy screamed.

More than anything at that moment, Mackie wished he had forced the girl's grandmother to listen to him, to go with him and seek out the Resistance, to join them and find somewhere underground where they could wait this out. It was their best chance, but few had thought the Syndicate would bother to invade small cities like Shiloh.

They were here, and it was go time.

Now that it was happening, they would have to listen to him. He shot out of his chair, grabbed the shotgun he had waiting, and stuck a pistol into his side-holster.

"Sammy, I'm coming for you!" He threw open the door and pounded on the next one over. "Open up! We're not safe here!"

"Stay the fuck away, aliens!" her grandma's harsh voice shouted. "You ain't probing shit here!"

What was her name? A damn fine time to forget. He pounded on the door and shouted, "It's your neighbor, Mackie, and we have to go NOW!"

Not waiting for another second, he kicked the door, and went sprawling backward. Damn, that wasn't as easy as the movies made it look. So instead he took a different tactic, and slammed the doorknob with the butt of his shotgun, until it fell off. He slammed the door this time with his shoulder, and it went flying open.

"Ahhh!" her grandma shouted, coming at him with a frying pan in one hand, a knife in the other.

"Whoa, whoa!" He took a step back. "It's me, Mackie!"

"GRANDMA!" Sammy shouted, jumping into her grandma's path with a book that she used to knock the knife aside. "It's our neighbor and he wants to help."

Her grandma paused, breathing in short, raspy breaths, but seemed to finally look at Mackie now.

"The fuck you doing breaking down our door?" she demanded.

"You need to watch your mouth around your granddaughter," he motioned to her, "and we need to get out of here, now. I know a place, so come on."

"It's too late for me," Sammy said. "I'm a fucking lost cause at this point. Plus, I mean, aliens… right? Do a couple swear words really matter?"

"She's mature for her age," her grandma offered, and glanced back outside as the building shook again. "This place you're talking, it's underground."

He nodded enthusiastically.

"Then stop playing with yourself and get us the hell out of here."

He motioned to Sammy with exasperation. "Really?"

"I'm with her," Sammy said. "Get a move on."

He laughed and shook his head. It was what he loved about Quinn, that and the memory of the time their hands had brushed at the market half a block over, that one time when they had both been reaching for the same box of soup. He knew from the bottom of his soul that the touch hadn't been an accident. It just couldn't have been. And so he worked hard to recreate that moment. It was why he made every effort to run into her in the halls. Her spunk, her playful attitude, and then there was the way that she always made him believe it could someday be possible. Sure, she did that with just a look, but he knew it would happen for them, eventually.

That is, it would if they all survived this, and right now that was looking rather doubtful.

"Just try to stay with me," he said, spinning from the room and leading them back out into the hallway.

"Your grannie falls, you're carrying her, not me," he said, realizing it was a dick move the moment the words left his mouth.

"Works for me," Sammy said. "As long as you know that

if you fall, tough shit."

"Hey," he stopped at the corner, peering around to see half the building missing, "what'd we say about language?"

The little nine-year-old stuck her tongue out at him, but her eyes went wide when she saw the missing wall and torn apart apartments that showed through. Rocket-launchers were going off, aimed at the alien ships, and the sound of semi-automatic rifles carried from a distance.

Either the Marines or the Resistance were putting up a fight.

Grandma caught up a moment later, huffing and out of breath, and when she saw what they were looking at she held Sammy close. "Whoever the hell you are, mister," she said, a finger pointed at Mackie's chest, "get us out of here. NOW."

Mackie just stared at her, then slowly shook his head. "I'm your neighbor, Mackie. I've lived next to you for, what, three years? Me and your daughter—"

"Let me stop you right there, because I highly doubt any sentence coming out of your mouth that relates to you and my daughter. And because you're rambling, when sticking around here could mean our death at any minute."

"But you do know me?"

She just glared.

"Fine, fine." He motioned for them to move on, and they all ran for the stairs. It was only four flights down, but he hadn't counted on an old woman slowing him down. Truthfully, he had half expected her to die of a heart attack the moment the invasion began.

A man ran past, ducking into a hallway, when the sound of shooting sounded, then a thud.

"Keep moving," Mackie hissed, motioning them downward.

At the ground floor, he turned and picked up grandma, helping her down the last two steps. With a tilt of his head and a wink, he kept on, ignoring the mutterings of "Was that necessary?" from behind.

The back door was already open and Sammy was halfway out, when Mackie darted forward and pulled her back just as a plasma blast hit the door and melted it away. More gunshots and an explosion later, and he poked his head out to see a group of men in dirty old cammies was firing on one of their invaders.

"GO!" he shouted, and took off for the alley opposite them.

"Where're you taking us?" Sammy asked, catching up to him. They reached the alley and had to turn and wait for grandma to reach them.

He was about to say something, but she must have anticipated it because she gave him the finger and said, "So this is your plan? Lead us outside so we're easier targets."

"We get underground, the Resistance will know what to do."

"Those terrorists? Those traitorous bastards?"

"Those would-be liberators and heroes," Mackie corrected her. "The only people around with underground networks where we might be able to hide."

He spun, searching for the path he'd seen them go when last he'd met with a Resistance representative. They had turned away and departed the moment he had said he wasn't ready, but he had been sure to find out where they returned to. It was simply more of a necessity that he keep Sammy safe, for now.

Another explosion overhead, and it looked like the Resistance had scored a hit against the Syndicate! The moment of joy was short-lived, however, as a new wave of Syndicate warriors arrived moments later in their blood-red armor, and had the nearby street cleared of resistance within mere moments.

Then, across the little square they now found themselves at, two retreating Resistance fighters went running.

"There!" Mackie said, motioning so the others could see. One was bald and the other had short hair cropped on the sides and combed to the side. They were on the retreat, and one had paused to kneel down beside a section of wall close to the floor.

He sprinted over and, before the two fighters could slip within and close the door, he was there, holding it open and the fighters looked up at him with terror and confusion.

"I'm your newest recruit," he said, glancing at the other the girl and grandma approaching. "We need shelter."

"A little late to the fight, pal," the bald one said, and then slipped inside, but the other nodded, and held open the door for all to enter.

BRRRT! A line of bullets hit between them and they all fell back and away from the door, looking up to see a Syndicate warrior in all red, his face covered in a red mask with silvery, shining glass over his face. A symbol like a snake eating itself was on his chest, and a rifle was pressed up against his shoulder.

Mackie put himself between the warrior and Sammy, while the Resistance fighter unslung his rifle and started firing at the warrior. Bullets bounced off of the red armor, and the warrior just kept coming.

"Get inside!" Mackie shouted, but when he looked, it was only her grandma. Her eyes went wide, and she pointed.

Sammy had run around back of the warrior and, to their horror, was running toward him. She leaped with a shout, distracting the warrior, who turned to look behind himself just as she slid between his legs and came out the other side, both hands on his rifle.

She yanked, and for a moment Mackie thought she might actually get it. Of course, the warrior was too strong, yanking the rifle back, about to slam it down on the little girl, when she hesitated.

In that moment, the Resistance fighter had managed to charge and shouted, "Down!"

The girl ducked and he unloaded on the Syndicate warrior, but the warrior just smirked and turned to him, then lifted his weapon to shoot—what he hadn't seen was that Mackie had come around to the other side, darted forward, and jammed the end of his shotgun up back of the Syndicate warrior's helmet.

"Never hit little girls, asshole," he said, and then pulled the trigger.

Helmet and all went flying, blood splattering, and Mackie just had enough time to snatch Sammy away and shelter her with his body before he heard the splat of brain matter falling to the ground.

"Get inside!" the Resistance fighter hissed, and this time there was no hesitation, aside from the moment, just before entering, when Mackie looked back and saw again what he thought for sure he couldn't have seen mere moments ago. A face he recognized all too well… one he couldn't believe for a second he was actually seeing, because if he was, none of this was worth fighting for—Quinn herself.

No, he convinced himself as he dropped down after Sammy and found her grandma and the other Resistance fighter waiting.

"What happened?" the bald man demanded. "They can't be down here."

"Believe me," the other said, glancing over to Mackie and then Sammy with a newfound level of respect, "they've earned their place, and damn sure proven themselves."

The bald man frowned, considered his companion, then nodded and stuck out a hand. "Welcome then, to the Resistance."

Mackie shook the hand, still in a daze over what had happened, and the fact that his obsession over saving Quinn's daughter *and* joining the Resistance were both fulfilled in one moment.

A glance at Sammy revealed she wasn't impressed, and was apparently as troubled as he was.

"You saw her too?" he asked.

She nodded, hesitated, and then shook her head. "No, my mom wouldn't betray us. She wouldn't. Get out there, kick some alien butt, and find her. You promise me."

"I promise," Mackie said, and then turned to follow the other two fighters to fulfill his destiny. First step, get the daughter on your side—check. Next, save the world, and get Quinn to go on a date with him… Maybe harder goals, but he meant to see them through nonetheless.

The Syndicate had just better get the fuck out of his way.

JUSTIN SLOAN SOCIAL

For a chance to see ALL of Justin's different Book Series
Check out his website below!

Website:
http://JustinSloanAuthor.com

Email List:
http://JustinSloanAuthor.com/Newsletter

Facebook Here:
https://www.facebook.com/JustinSloanAuthor

MICHAEL ANDERLE SOCIAL

Website:
http://kurtherianbooks.com/

Email List:
http://kurtherianbooks.com/email-list/

Facebook Here:
https://www.facebook.com/TheKurtherianGambitBooks/

STORIES BY JUSTIN SLOAN

CURSED NIGHT

Hounds of God
Hounds of Light

FALLS OF REDEMPTION (TRILOGY)

Land of Gods
Retribution Calls
Tears of Devotion

RECLAIMING HONOR (A KURTHERIAN GAMBIT SERIES)

Justice is Calling (Audiobook available)
Claimed By Honor (Audiobook coming soon)
Judgment Has Fallen (Audiobook coming)
Angel of Reckoning (Audiobook coming)

MODERN NECROMANCY (TRILOGY)

Death Marked
Death Bound
Death Crowned

ALLIE STROM (TRILOGY)

Allie Strom and the Ring of Solomon
Allie Strom and the Sword of the Spirit
Allie Strom and the Tenth Worthy

STORIES BY MICHAEL ANDERLE

KURTHERIN GAMBIT SERIES TITLES INCLUDE:

FIRST ARC

Death Becomes Her (01) - Queen Bitch (02) - Love Lost (03) - Bite This (04) - Never Forsaken (05) - Under My Heel (06) - Kneel Or Die (07)

SECOND ARC

We Will Build (08) - It's Hell To Choose (09) - Release The Dogs of War (10) - Sued For Peace (11) - We Have Contact (12) - My Ride is a Bitch (13) - Don't Cross This Line (14)

THIRD ARC *(Due 2017)*

Never Submit (15) - Never Surrender (16) - Forever Defend (17) - Might Makes Right (18) - Ahead Full (19) - Capture Death (20) - Life Goes On (21)

New Series

THE SECOND DARK AGES

(Michael's Return)

The Dark Messiah (01)
The Darkest Night (02)

THE BORIS CHRONICLES

With Paul C. Middleton

Evacuation
Retaliation
Revelation
Restitution (*2017*)

RECLAIMING HONOR

With Justin Sloan

Justice Is Calling (01)
Claimed By Honor (02)
Judgment Has Fallen (03)

THE ETHERIC ACADEMY

With TS Paul

ALPHA CLASS (01)
ALPHA CLASS (02) (*02/03 2017*)
ALPHA CLASS (03) (*05/06 2017*)

TERRY HENRY "TH" WALTON CHRONICLES

With Craig Martelle

Nomad Found (01)
Nomad Redeemed (02)
Nomad Unleashed (03)
Nomad Fury (04)

TRIALS AND TRIBULATIONS

With Natalie Grey

Risk Be Damned (01)
Damned to Hell (02) coming soon
Hell's Worst Nightmare (03) coming soon

SHORT STORIES

Frank Kurns Stories of the Unknownworld 01 (*7.5*)
You Don't Mess with John's Cousin

Frank Kurns Stories of the Unknownworld 02 (*9.5*)
Bitch's Night Out

Frank Kurns Stories of the Unknownworld 03 (13.25)
With Natalie Grey
BELLATRIX

RISE OF MAGIC

With CM Raymond and LE Barbant

Restriction (01)
Reawakening (02)

AUDIOBOOKS

Available at Audible.com and iTunes

The Kurtherian Gambit

Death Becomes Her - Available Now
Queen Bitch – Available Now
Love Lost – Available Now

Reclaiming Honor Series

Justice Is Calling – Available Now
Claimed By Honor – Available Now

TERRY HENRY "TH" WALTON CHRONICLES

Nomad Found
Nomad Redeemed - Coming Soon

THE ETHERIC ACADEMY

Alpha Class
Alpha Class 2 - Coming soon

ANTHOLOGIES

Glimpse
Honor in Death
(Michael's First Few Days)

Beyond the Stars: At Galaxy's Edge
Tabitha's Vacation

46873742R00133

Made in the USA
Middletown, DE
11 August 2017